ABOUT THE BOOK

An earthquake in Square Toe territory! And Miss Pickerell, the winds howling all around and the steering wheel of her old automobile shaking in her hands, is off to find the earthquake specialists who have mysteriously disappeared.

Following a map drawn by her middle nephew, Euphus, she lands first in an abandoned cave, then in an elevator that groans its way down a narrow shaft 9,100 feet beneath the earth's surface, where scientists carrying out secret experiments mistake her for a spy.

But Miss Pickerell does not give up. How can she when she thinks of Nancy Agatha, her cow, and Pumpkins, her cat, waiting in the trailer near the cave, and of her seven nieces and nephews and all the other animals and people who must be saved?

In this, her eleventh adventure, Miss Pickerell has to use all her courage and wits—and her #11 crochet hook—to avert disasters on her beloved mountains.

Miss Pickerell to the
EARTHQUAKE
Rescue

Miss Pickerell to the
EARTHQUAKE
Rescue

Ellen MacGregor and Dora Pantell

Illustrated by Charles Geer

NEW YORK ● ST. LOUIS ● SAN FRANCISCO ● AUCKLAND
DÜSSELDORF ● JOHANNESBURG ● BOGOTÁ ● LONDON
MADRID ● MEXICO ● MONTREAL ● NEW DELHI ● PANAMA ● PARIS
SÃO PAULO ● SINGAPORE ● SYDNEY ● TOKYO ● TORONTO

All characters in this book are entirely fictitious.

Library of Congress Cataloging in Publication Data

MacGregor, Ellen.
    Miss Pickerell to the earthquake rescue.

    SUMMARY: Earthquakes in a nearby county and the disappearance of two earthquake-prevention scientists bring Miss Pickerell on the run to tackle the crises.
    [1. Earthquakes—Fiction] I. Pantell, Dora F., joint author. II. Geer, Charles. III. Title.
PZ7.M1698Mqd   [Fic]   76-52447
ISBN 0-07-044586-9
ISBN 0-07-044587-7 lib. bdg.

FOR PAMELA LYNN AND HER VETERINARIAN
GRANDFATHER, WHO ADORE PUMPKINS AND THE
COW AND ALL ANIMALS, GREAT AND SMALL—

Contents

1

A MATTER OF OPINION

Miss Pickerell pushed her eyeglasses a little farther down on her nose and peered over them at the bowling ball in her hands. It didn't feel very comfortable there. The bowling shoes she was wearing didn't fit right, either. She sighed deeply.

"We're waiting for you, Miss Pickerell," a voice from a far corner of the bowling alley called out. "The cameras are ready to shoot."

Miss Pickerell lifted her hands, the ball tightly clutched between them, to shield her eyes against the glaring klieg lights. She searched out the far corner. The young man who had spoken stood leaning against a television camera. He had thick blond hair and long, dark brown

11

sideburns. His name, she knew, was Alfonse Quest. A very tall, thin young girl stood next to him. She was wearing a cap with a visor brim that hung over her face and purple pants that were tucked into hip-length boots. Miss Pickerell couldn't imagine why. The weather was warm and sunny on this late summer morning.

The young man spoke again.

"Miss Pickerell," he said, "the cameraman on the other side is waiting for my signal. Shall I tell him that you're ready?"

Miss Pickerell steadied the ball against her right hip and with her free hand tucked a loose hairpin firmly into place. She had a good mind to tell Mr. Quest her full opinion of him. On second thought, she decided against it.

"Yes," she murmured, lifting the ball again. "I'm ready."

She glanced briefly at her friend, Professor Humwhistel, who had left his work at the space laboratory to give her courage in the bowling alley, and at her seven nieces and nephews, all lined up on wooden stools against the right-hand wall. Rosemary, her oldest niece, was leading her brothers and sisters in a cheer.

"Hip! Hip! Hurray!" they shouted.

"A strike!" Euphus, her middle nephew, leaning over a score sheet in front of him, screamed. "Wipe out all ten pins, Aunt Lavinia!"

Miss Pickerell drew in her breath, closed her eyes, and aimed.

"Forevermore!" she whispered as the ball went sailing down the lane and into the gutter.

Her seven nieces and nephews let out a very long sigh. Professor Humwhistel applauded weakly. Miss Pickerell paid no attention.

"I hope," she called out decisively, "I hope, Mr. Alfonse Quest, that I may finally stop this nonsense."

Mr. Quest did not answer immediately. He wiped his forehead with a large white handkerchief that he took out of his plaid jacket pocket. Then he walked over to Miss Pickerell. She observed that his eyebrows had practically climbed up to his hairline.

"Mr. Quest," she told him before he had a chance to say a single word, "I can see that you want me to do what you call *still another camera take*. The answer is *no*."

Mr. Quest swallowed visibly.

"I know for a fact," Miss Pickerell continued, "that the last picture you snapped of me was picture number sixteen. I know because I've counted carefully. And I took the five running

13

steps forward, stopping just short of the yellow line exactly the way you instructed me to do. That was the pose you wanted, I believe."

Mr. Quest swallowed again, this time so hard that his Adam's apple seemed about to pop out of his throat.

"I can also tell you," Miss Pickerell went on, as she sat down on the bench behind her and began changing her shoes, "I can very definitely tell you that I have no intention of remaining in this bowling alley for another instant. My cow and my cat have been waiting outside in the trailer long enough. And I have more important things to do on my farm."

She adjusted another loose hairpin and picked her knitting bag up from the floor. Today was her day for polishing brasses. If she left the bowling alley right away, she reflected, she could be driving up the private lane that led to Square Toe Farm in less than an hour. She would have just enough time to finish the polishing she had started before breakfast and to begin rearranging her rock collection. Some of the labels had come off when they were at the State Fair. The Governor apologized when he returned them but, he explained, he really couldn't do anything to help. He wasn't sure which rocks came from Mars and which from the moon. Miss Pickerell walked toward the exit, feeling very good about the prospect of sorting out her rocks and making fresh labels for them.

Mr. Quest and the girl with the cap were at the door ahead of her. The girl spread out her arms and blocked the way. Miss Pickerell remembered that her name was Mina Minor and that she worked for a company called Bowling Forever or some such silly thing.

"I cannot let you do this," the girl was saying now, while she nervously pushed her cap back so that a lot of curly red hair fell down over her face. "My employer would never permit it."

Miss Pickerell gasped. She had never heard of such impertinence.

"May I remind you, Miss Minor," she said icily, "that I agreed to bowl on your marathon television show for the sake of the earthquake victims of Cross Finger County. I repeat, for the earthquake victims of Cross Finger County. I have no interest in your Bowling Forever Company."

"Bowling for Beauty, Now and Forever, and Company," Mr. Quest corrected. "They are sponsoring this marathon, Miss Pickerell. Without them, there would be no money for air time. There . . ."

"And we asked you to appear," Miss Minor broke in, "because we knew people would watch if you were on the screen. You're a celebrity, Miss Pickerell. You've been to Mars and the moon and the weather satellite and everybody has heard of you. And you brought back all those rocks. And you ate in the moon cafeteria. And you . . ."

Miss Pickerell shrugged her shoulders impatiently. She had never really wanted to go to any of those places so far away from her beloved farm and animals. She didn't honestly know how she always got mixed up in such outlandish adventures. At the moment, she wished she could open the door and just walk out.

Miss Minor was still talking.

"Your bowling demonstration will be on the screen every ten minutes," she was saying. "So you see, Miss Pickerell, your performance has to be perfect."

Miss Pickerell nearly laughed out loud. Did Mr. Quest and Miss Minor think she was a champion? And why a demonstration every ten minutes? That was both unnecessary and silly. She said as much, vigorously, to Miss Minor.

"But Miss Pickerell," Miss Minor exclaimed, "You are doing the commercial! Didn't you know? First you bowl and then we talk about our bowling balls and our bowling pins and our bowling shoes and our . . ."

Miss Pickerell stared, dumbfounded. She couldn't believe her ears. This . . . this was too much. This was impossible. Personally, she didn't much care for television. But she had absolutely *no* respect for commercials. She was always telling her oldest niece, Rosemary, and her middle nephew, Euphus, her opinion. Rosemary and Euphus just laughed. They knew every commercial by heart, practically.

She could hear them singing their latest favorite now as they made their way toward her. Professor Humwhistel was behind them. He was trying to shake the ashes out of his pipe into a paper drinking cup that he was carrying. They were falling instead onto his old-fashioned wool bow tie and all over his tightly buttoned black-and-white-checked vest.

"I have been outside to talk to your animals, Miss Pickerell," he said, as soon as he reached her. "I told them you would be there soon."

"Thank you, Professor," Miss Pickerell said. "I am going to them now."

Mr. Quest groaned. Miss Minor threw up her hands in despair. Miss Pickerell squared her shoulders.

"Under no circumstances," she said, shuddering at the very thought, "will I stay to put my feet together, crouch down, hold that heavy ball close to my right knee, and then take those five running steps forward all over again. For the purpose *I* had in mind, that of raising money for earthquake victims, my bowling is quite good enough. Don't you agree, Professor?"

Professor Humwhistel cleared his throat before answering.

"I hope you will not be offended, Miss Pickerell," he said, "but I was only half watching. I was thinking about earthquakes and their causes. It's rather a complicated subject."

"I learned all about earthquakes in my science class last year," said Euphus.

"Yes?" Professor Humwhistel asked in an interested tone.

Miss Pickerell smiled. She was very proud of her middle nephew, Euphus. She was especially proud of the fact that he was so good in science. But he had a way of chattering on and on when he had a chance. She hoped Professor Humwhistel would not encourage him to say too much now. Personally, she was too tired to listen to either of them. She walked back to the bench to pick up her umbrella.

"I learned first of all," said Euphus, following her instantly, "that the earth has been changing all these millions of years and that some of the changes produced our mountains and our continents."

"Right," Professor Humwhistel, following just as closely, agreed. "The earth was once only a ball of flaming gases and molten liquids, surrounded by a rock crust. The core of the earth has still not cooled down."

"What about earthquakes?" Miss Pickerell asked, intent on getting them both back to the point and sitting down to listen.

"Well," Euphus continued, "when there is a lot of strain on the rock crusts, they break. A crustal break is also called a fault. The breaks bring on the shaking of the earth, which is called an earthquake."

Professor Humwhistel nodded.

"That's correct, Euphus," he said, "but perhaps a little oversimplified. Earthquakes may occur for a number of reasons. For example, great blocks of rock along fault areas may slip because of pressure and bend and eventually rip apart. One of these fault areas stretches across part of Square Toe County."

"I know, I know," Euphus exclaimed. "It's on the other side of the mountain, where the men are always measuring with their . . . their . . ."

"Seismographs," Professor Humwhistel said. "There have been a number of interesting earthquake studies, though only recently with seismograph instruments. As an example, I can tell you that the earthquake in 1755—or was it 1756—and also, the one, more recently, closer to home, both had . . ."

It was Professor Humwhistel who was now talking on and on. He talked about causes of earthquakes and types of earthquakes and about their various differences and their frequent similarities. Miss Pickerell felt a rising wave of exasperation as she listened. Not *once* did he say anything about how to *prevent* an earthquake. Why, her blood practically boiled when she thought of all the suffering people and animals and wildlife made homeless by the earthquake and its terrible floods in Cross Finger County. Some snakes, she knew, were able to swim. But what about the baby birds who couldn't, who were too young to fly very high? And what about the cats and dogs and horses and cows and lambs who needed to be led and carried out of the flooded places? And the people not knowing where to run? And the babies, too weak and frightened, some of them, even to cry? There had to be a way of avoiding these terrible things. There simply *had* to be!

Something she had once read about earth-quakes was running through her head. Something about the prevention of earthquakes. Was it by the pouring in of water? She couldn't remember. She couldn't recall where she had read it, either. But she had *every* intention of finding out. *Somebody* had to do something to prevent so much suffering . . .

Miss Minor's voice, sounding almost desperate now, broke in on her thoughts.

"Miss Pickerell," she was saying, as she nervously pushed her hair away from her face, "Mr. Quest and I have had a long conference. We have made a decision. If you would agree to do one more shot, only one, I promise you . . ."

Miss Pickerell looked up. She could see clearly now that the girl had soft blue eyes and that she was wearing false eyelashes, which were unevenly attached.

Miss Pickerell suddenly felt sorry for her. She sat back wearily and changed once more into the bowling shoes. Then, moving almost like an automaton, she stepped over to the lane, picked up the ball, took the five steps forward, and leaning low, sent it rolling. Without even a glance down the lane and ignoring the crash of the pins, she returned to the bench.

"Perfect!" Mr. Quest shouted, instantly running over to shake her hand. "Perfect! Perfect! Perfect!"

"You knocked down every pin!" Miss Minor, also running, called. "You should be very happy."

"I would be much happier," Miss Pickerell said tersely, "if I could do something to prevent an earthquake."

"Oh, that!" said Miss Minor.

"Impossible!" added Mr. Quest.

Miss Pickerell's eyebrows rose.

"You think so?" she asked.

"Why, of course," Miss Minor replied, nodding her head so emphatically that her cap fell off and Mr. Quest had to bend down to pick it up for her.

"We can only help the victims," he said when he was standing upright again. "It's all anyone can do."

Miss Pickerell threw him a scornful look.

"That," she said dryly, "is strictly a matter of opinion."

She stooped to tie up her shoelace, tucked a few more loose hairpins into place, and marched toward the door, leaving Mr. Quest staring at her and Miss Minor, her mouth open, reaching for the eyelashes that were unmistakably dropping down onto her cheeks.

2

A STRANGE DISAPPEARANCE

Professor Humwhistel and Euphus followed Miss Pickerell across the street to her automobile. Rosemary said that she was expecting an important telephone call from her best girl friend and she would go home with Dwight, her oldest brother, and all the smaller children, in Dwight's old station wagon.

Miss Pickerell walked over to the trailer first, to see how her animals were getting along. The trailer had a red-and-white-striped awning, with fringes all around, to protect Nancy Agatha, the cow, and Pumpkins, Miss Pickerell's big black cat, from too much sun or unexpected rain or snow. Miss Pickerell seldom went anywhere without her animals and she wanted them to be well and happy.

"Thank you again, Professor Humwhistel," she said, "for going out to talk to them. It helped put my mind at ease."

"Not at all," Professor Humwhistel replied, while he finished securing his motorcycle to the back door of the trailer. He courteously helped Miss Pickerell into her automobile and joined her in the front seat. Pumpkins jumped over from the trailer to sit in his lap. And Euphus lay down next to the cow. Nancy Agatha mooed contentedly.

Miss Pickerell made certain that all the doors were safely locked. Then she let out the clutch, shifted gears with a jerk, and steered forward in the direction of the highway. She threaded her way between and around the new buses that now jammed Square Toe City's main streets. She was still fuming over the idea of appearing on national television in a bowling commercial and she had little patience with traffic tie-ups. A number of times, she was sorely tempted to blow her horn, even though she knew it was against the law except in an emergency.

Once they were out in the open country, she threw all caution to the winds and drove faster and faster. Professor Humwhistel watched the needle of the speedometer rise to twenty, then to twenty-five, then to thirty miles an hour. Miss Pickerell had to laugh when she saw the startled look on his face.

"You needn't worry, Professor," she said. "My limit is still thirty-five."

"I wasn't worried," Professor Humwhistel assured her.

"Neither was I," Euphus piped up from the trailer.

Miss Pickerell turned briefly to ask him please not to interrupt. She had made up her mind to come directly to the point with Professor Humwhistel about earthquake prevention and she wanted no distractions.

"Professor," she said, "I once read an article discussing the possibility of pumping water, I believe, into a fault to prevent the occurrence of major earthquakes."

"It was water," Professor Humwhistel answered instantly. "The article about this possibility appeared in a Sunday newspaper about eleven months ago. It suggested the slow pumping of water down along the earthquake rift, where the faults lie."

"I understand, Professor," Miss Pickerell said, although she was not entirely sure that she did. "Please go on."

"The hope was," Professor Humwhistel continued, "that the introduction of water would relieve the pressure on the earth's crust and prevent major faults or fractures. There would still be some tremors, but they would be harmless."

Miss Pickerell nodded for the professor to proceed.

"You see," he said, "the earth's interior consists of a core, a mantle, and a crust. The crust is a relatively thin layer of rock covering the earth."

He paused to puff on his half-lit pipe.

"I am following you very well," Miss Pickerell prompted.

"Good," said Professor Humwhistel between puffs. "Earthquakes may occur when the near-surface rocks, that is the rocks in the earth's crust, break apart to accommodate the up-swelling liquid rock."

"Up-swelling liquid rock?" Miss Pickerell repeated.

"You remember, Miss Pickerell," Professor Humwhistel explained, "that I told you how the core of the earth is still not cooled down. The earth has gradually changed, as Euphus mentioned. It is no longer only a ball of flaming gases

and liquids. But there is still that hot liquid rock under the crust."

Miss Pickerell was thinking hard. She was thinking so hard that she actually stopped the car and then, realizing that she was on a highway, rushed to start it up again.

"I don't quite see, Professor," she said, "what this talk of liquid rock has to do with the idea of water that you just spoke of. Or even with the idea of the blocks of rocks bending and breaking that you talked about in the bowling alley."

Professor Humwhistel did not answer immediately. He seemed to be collecting his thoughts.

"It is important to remember the essential point that Euphus brought up," he said finally, "the point that breaks in the earth's rock crust have something to do with an earthquake. The earthquake may be major or minor, depending on the degree of the break."

"But where do these breaks occur?" Miss Pickerell asked.

"Generally, in two kinds of places," the professor told her. "One is along the edges of crustal plates where the six major plates and the smaller plates that make up the earth's outer shell can get stuck. Then they bump into each other or slide past each other too suddenly and this can cause an earthquake. Another place is along a crack within the plate where the pressure of rock under strain can also cause an earthquake."

Miss Pickerell thought the explanation was a little incomplete. *"Something* must make the plates slide, Professor," she argued. *"Something* must also build up the pressure. What is that?"

"Those are very good questions," Professor Humwhistel said, smiling. "There are a number of theories about the answers. Perhaps differences in temperature, differences, that is, between the white-hot region near the center of the earth and the cooler region near the crust. They can set off currents of hot, molten rock."

"Oh?" Miss Pickerell exclaimed.

"Perhaps loading the earth's crust with too much water in some places," Professor Humwhistel continued. "Perhaps radioactive heating. Perhaps . . ."

"Stop! Please stop, Professor," Miss Pickerell pleaded, wishing her hands were free so that she could put them over her ears. "I'll never remember."

Professor Humwhistel refilled his pipe. They rode on in silence. Every once in awhile, Miss Pickerell looked out across Square Toe Mountain in the direction of Cross Finger County. She was glad that it was far enough away so that she didn't actually have to see the suffering. Of course, she had seen the pictures in the papers—the houses torn apart, the barns where the roof beams had caved in, the people, their eyes full of terror, running on ground that seemed to be coming apart under their feet. She shivered and steered the automobile off the highway.

"Where are we going?" Euphus called out.

"To Mr. Rugby's diner for some tea," Miss Pickerell told him. "I feel cold."

"Swell!" Euphus shouted. "I can have some peppermintade."

Professor Humwhistel commented that he would have some peppermintade, too.

"By the way, Miss Pickerell," he added, "I forgot to mention that two of my colleagues from the Science Institute are currently engaged in an earthquake-prevention research project, somewhere not too far from here. Project Waterfowl, I believe it is called."

"Project Waterfowl!" Euphus laughed. "What a crazy name!"

"Well, I may not have gotten it right," Professor Humwhistel admitted. "In any case, they left four months ago."

"Four months!" Euphus exclaimed. "Wow!"

"Yes!" Miss Pickerell exclaimed, too. "They must surely have made some progress by now."

Professor Humwhistel looked glum.

"I don't know," he replied. "They have not been heard from since."

Euphus whistled and said "Wow" again.

"I have written repeatedly, care of the Science Institute, Special Attention: Seismology Institute," the professor went on. "I have been advised that the letters have been forwarded. But there has been no reply."

"Well!" Miss Pickerell said indignantly. "I must say they certainly have bad manners. I would go so far as to call it inexcusably bad manners."

Professor Humwhistel said nothing. He did not speak until they saw the sign outside Mr. Rugby's diner, announcing: MOON-BURGERS AND ECLIPSE SPECIALS. M. Rugby, formerly with THE MOON CAF-ETERIA, Proprietor.

"I wish it were only a matter of manners, Miss Pickerell," he said then. And, as he helped her out of the car, he added grimly, "They seem, I'm afraid, actually to have disappeared."

3

THE ABANDONED CAVE

Mr. Rugby's diner was very crowded. News about the taste of his eclipse specials had spread far and wide and customers came from all over. Mr. Esticott, on vacation from his job as Square Toe City's baggage master, was serving at the counter. And Mr. Kettelson, the hardware-store man, who gloomily complained that people had stopped buying pots and pans altogether lately, was helping to wait on tables. He wore a starched white waiter's jacket with a red artificial flower in the lapel. His tired face lit up when he saw Miss Pickerell and he rushed over to escort her and Professor Humwhistel and Euphus to a booth. But Mr. Rugby, his double chins bouncing with excitement, his tall chef's hat bobbing up and down, raced ahead of him.

"Good afternoon, Miss Pickerell," he said, nearly tripping over the apron that was much too long for him. "Good afternoon to you, too, Professor Humwhistel and Euphus. How did the bowling go, Miss Pickerell? I wanted to be there to applaud but, as you can see, it was impossible for me to leave my diner. Plain impossible!"

He glanced quickly around the room, said, "Hah!" and led them to the large round table in the center, the one he ordinarily reserved for the Governor to sit at when he was in from the State Capital.

"Nothing is too good for you, Miss Pickerell," he added, as he pulled out a chair for her and pushed it in again, after she had sat down.

Miss Pickerell noticed that the table was covered with a red plush cloth, trimmed near the edges with flowers like the one Mr. Kettelson wore on his uniform. She made a mental note to tell Mr. Rugby the next time she saw him alone that plush was most uneconomical as a table-cloth. He could certainly not put it in the washing machine. And cleaning bills were very high these days. She made another mental note to be sure to see to it that Euphus did not spill any of his peppermintade on the table.

35

Mr. Rugby's jaw dropped at least two inches when Miss Pickerell asked for the peppermintades for Euphus and Professor Humwhistel and the cup of tea for herself.

"Impossible!" he said again. "You cannot leave my diner without something more substantial. I will bring three lunches with the peppermintades and the tea."

Miss Pickerell felt a little more relaxed after she ate.

"Tell me about your friends, Professor Humwhistel," she asked. "The two who are studying earthquake prevention."

"They are very learned gentlemen," Professor Humwhistel replied.

"Humph!" Miss Pickerell commented, thinking about the way they ignored the professor's letters.

"Dr. Donner has won many prizes for his work in the field of seismology, which, as you know, is the study of earthquakes," the professor stated. "Dr. Blitzenkrieg, recently retired from the Navy, has a worldwide reputation. He has been concentrating lately on the development of seismographs which will measure and record the earth's vibrations more accurately so that . . ."

He broke off as the hardware-store man, no longer wearing the waiter's jacket, approached. Mr. Kettelson explained that he was not on duty anymore since Mr. Rugby's regular afternoon waiter had arrived.

"And how is your cow?" he hastened to ask Miss Pickerell. "I have not seen her in a few days."

"Frankly, Mr. Kettelson," Miss Pickerell replied, "I would have been much happier if Mr. Rugby had given us our seats in a booth near the window. I could have kept an eye on her there."

Mr. Kettelson craned his long, thin neck over the tables between him and the open window.

"She looks fine to me," he reported. "Pumpkins is playing with her tail."

He sat down next to Euphus.

"We were just talking about earthquakes," Miss Pickerell told him. "Two of Professor Humwhistel's friends are studying earthquake prevention."

"Terrible, terrible, what is happening in Cross Finger County!" Mr. Kettelson exclaimed. "They showed some more pictures on the eleven o'clock news. I saw a boy trying to rescue his dog while . . ."

"Please!" Miss Pickerell begged, tightly pressing her hands against her ears. "I can't bear to hear about it."

"Did he save the dog?" Euphus wanted to know.

Mr. Kettelson looked at Miss Pickerell and ignored the question.

"I was just wondering," he said, as he sorrowfully shook his head, "how long it will be before Square Toe County is hit by an earthquake."

Miss Pickerell gulped down the remaining drops of tea in her cup.

"What makes you think Square Toe County will be hit, Mr. Kettelson?" she asked, while she quickly comforted herself with the knowledge that Mr. Kettelson had a pessimistic view about practically everything.

"It stands to reason," Mr. Kettelson said sadly. "Cross Finger County is situated on one fault. Square Toe County is situated on another. One may be as bad as the other. For all we know, one may even be an extension of the other."

Miss Pickerell looked to Professor Humwhistel for reassurance. He murmured something about probability curves and detection systems. She waited for him to tell her something less vague. But he only proceeded to blow on the rimless eyeglasses that he wore on a black silk ribbon attached to the top button of his vest. After he finished blowing, he wiped the glasses with his handkerchief. Miss Pickerell beckoned to the afternoon waiter and ordered more tea. "Professor Humwhistel," she asked then, "just where did you say your friends went to do their studying?"

"I didn't say," Professor Humwhistel replied. "I didn't say because I'm not entirely sure. I believe it was to an abandoned cave."

"A cave!" Euphus shouted and added "Excuse me" when he saw Miss Pickerell about to give him a sharp look.

"You see," Professor Humwhistel explained, "if they have to do any experimenting deep in the earth, maybe even twenty-five thousand feet down, the best place is far away from houses and people."

Miss Pickerell, who had, from time to time, seen and heard the digging that the electric company did on the streets of Square Toe City, couldn't agree more. She nodded her head emphatically.

"And this cave, I understand," Professor Humwhistel continued, "is already very deep down in the earth, deep enough for . . ."

Miss Pickerell couldn't keep herself from interrupting.

"Professor Humwhistel," she questioned, "have you *any* ideas as to where this cave is?"

The professor took a fountain pen out of his pocket and began to draw a map on his napkin. Euphus leaned forward over the table to watch.

"This circle I am making now," Professor Humwhistel said, "is Square Toe City. And this circle across the mountain is Cross Finger County. The cave is about halfway between them, not too far from this smaller circle I am drawing to represent a place called Heatherbarrow City."

Euphus opened his mouth to say something and changed his mind.

"To get to the area of the cave," Professor Humwhistel went on, "you do not need to go far on the other side of the mountain and you do not actually have to enter Heatherbarrow City. There is a bypass on the far side of Square Toe City as you approach the middle road leading up to the other side of the mountain. The dots I am now drawing for you show where the bypass begins and how it proceeds to a deserted woody area, called unofficially, I believe, Winterwood Forest. The cave is somewhere in that forest. But, as I have mentioned, Miss Pickerell, I am not sure as to exactly . . ."

"I am!" Euphus burst out. "I mean I'm sure about where the cave is. I was there. Twice! When I was in the third grade. A long time ago."

Miss Pickerell, Professor Humwhistel, and Mr. Kettelson all gasped.

"My science teacher took us," Euphus added. "He used to take the children every year. But he doesn't do it anymore. He tells the kids it isn't safe."

"Why not?" Miss Pickerell asked instantly.

"Bombs!" Euphus answered just as quickly. "Missiles! Spies!"

Miss Pickerell gave him a long stare.

Euphus squirmed and leaned over the table again.

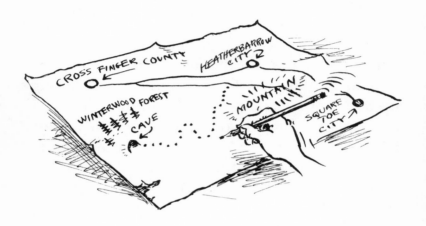

"Maybe I don't remember *exactly* about the reasons," he said. "But I *know* where the cave is."

He counted the dots on Professor Humwhistel's napkin. Then he took the professor's pen and added a few more of his own.

"First," he said, "you finish with Professor Humwhistel's fifteen dots. After that, you count up to seven on mine. And you count half a mile between every dot."

"And the cave is your seventh dot," Miss Pickerell repeated carefully.

Mr. Kettelson looked at her with sudden suspicion. He exchanged glances with Professor Humwhistel. Professor Humwhistel smiled at Miss Pickerell.

"Do you think," he asked, "that if you go to the cave, you will be able to accomplish more than Dr. Donner and Dr. Blitzenkrieg, Miss Pickerell?"

"You could disappear! Just like them!" Euphus exclaimed.

"And think of those bombs!" Mr. Kettelson added. "Those missiles! Most probably, even spies!!"

Miss Pickerell stared unseeingly at them.

"I didn't *say* I was going," she answered finally. "But I would certainly *like* to, if *only,* Professor Humwhistel, to give your Dr. Donner and Dr. Blitzenkrieg a lesson in manners. *And* in responsibility to their friends."

She picked up the second cup of tea that the afternoon waiter had long ago placed before her.

She drank it stone cold.

4
MISS PICKERELL
TAKES NO CHANCES

Euphus was unusually quiet on the ride from the diner. He sat in the trailer, writing on the back of one of Mr. Rugby's menus. Mr. Kettelson, who had decided to return to the farm with Miss Pickerell so that he could spend a little more time with the cow, always carried a few menus in his back pocket. He gave one to Euphus when he asked for some paper.

The minute he jumped out of the trailer, Euphus handed Miss Pickerell what he had written. She frowned at the spelling. But she read it aloud to Professor Humwhistel and Mr. Kettelson, mentally correcting the spelling as she went along:

Earthquakes

Causes

① Pressure of gases forcing volcanic rocks up and then the rocks break the crust.

② Blocks of rocks falling apart because of pressure.

③ Temperature variations in the earth's interior.

④ Too much or too little lubricant.

⑤ Too much water.

⑥ The six major plates getting stuck or hitting each other.

⑦ The rocks in the plates also hitting each other when they shift.

Prevenshun

① Releive the pressure in some way.

② Is that the same as #1 ??

③ I'll tell you tomorrow. It takes too long to write down.

④ That's easy — take some away or add just a little.

⑤ But the newspaper artical said to pump the water in ?!?

⑥ I'm not sure.

⑦ I'm not sure about this one either.

"Why, Euphus," she said, "I must say that when you pay attention, you have an excellent memory."

Professor Humwhistel and Mr. Kettelson both agreed. Professor Humwhistel offered to fill him in on the answers to #6 and #7, and to clarify his points #2 and #5 for him as soon as he unhitched his motorcycle from the trailer.

"I'd rather you taught me how to play chess now," Euphus said. "I want to be able to beat my father."

"Certainly," Professor Humwhistel answered.

He followed Euphus into the parlor, where Miss Pickerell kept one chess set, three checker sets, and a jigsaw puzzle with some of the pieces missing.

Mr. Kettelson gently led Nancy Agatha out of the trailer and said he would take her into the pasture.

"The upper pasture, please, Mr. Kettelson," Miss Pickerell told him. "It's cooler at this time of day."

With Pumpkins at her heels, Miss Pickerell walked into her kitchen. The quiet, sunny room was a relief after the dark, clattering bowling alley. Miss Pickerell looked around with pleasure at the big, square table and chairs that stood under the neatly curtained windows, at the newly planted geraniums in their bright red pots marching across the windowsills, at the yellow wall clock with the huge black numbers on it, even at the telephone which hung on the wall directly beneath the clock and next to her new freezer unit with the small radio on it. The brasses she had finished polishing lay on the counter top to the left of her sink. A kettle with a long, skinny spout, a very deep ashtray that Miss Pickerell used for stray safety pins, and a candlestick that Mr. Kettelson had brought her from his hardware store were on the right-hand counter, waiting to be attended to.

"Well, I'd better get to them," Miss Pickerell said to Pumpkins, who was sitting between two geranium pots, busily washing his face. He meowed his approval.

She looked up at the clock. It was just a few minutes after one. She could still catch *The Mrs. Beeton Cooking Hour* on the radio. It would be pleasant to follow while she was polishing.

As usual, Mrs. Beeton began her program by dusting some flour off her hands. Listeners could clearly hear her palms swishing against each other. Besides, Mrs. Beeton always explained everything that she did. "I must get this flour off my hands," she said at the start of each program.

Today, she was discussing an early-American

recipe for preparing boiled cauliflower. She talked for awhile about the importance of first sprinkling grated cheese over the cauliflower.

"It gives a special Italian touch," she explained.

Miss Pickerell, who couldn't help wondering how an Italian touch got into an early-American recipe, kept on polishing and listening.

Mrs. Beeton went on to her next step, that of grating the cheese at home. Miss Pickerell didn't think this part was at all practical. Store-bought grated cheese was just as good and much less trouble. She stopped listening while she inspected the kettle to make sure she could see her face in it and went to place it carefully on the shelf in the hallway next to the kitchen. Nancy Agatha's picture hung over the shelf. Miss Pickerell paused to admire it. Mr. Squeers, Square Toe City's photographer, had caught a very good likeness, she thought.

When Miss Pickerell returned to the kitchen, Mrs. Beeton was outlining the steps for cooking the cauliflower.

"I heartily recommend browning it before an open fire," she said. "There is really nothing like an open fire for bringing out the distinctive taste of this recipe. If you . . ."

The radio went dead in the middle of her sentence. A deep male voice replaced that of Mrs. Beeton's.

"We are sorry to interrupt *The Mrs. Beeton Cooking Hour,*" it announced, "but an important bulletin has just come in. An earthquake has erupted in Heatherbarrow City. Everything is being done to evacuate the residents as quickly as possible. The Governor has alerted the National Guard. Rescue teams have already . . ."

"Heatherbarrow City!" Miss Pickerell breathed. "That's *nearer* than Cross Finger County!"

Professor Humwhistel, muttering something about earthquake lines, stood in the kitchen doorway. Euphus, looking ready to burst with excitement, rushed over to make the radio louder. Mr. Kettelson, running his fingers through his few gray hairs, raced in from outside.

"Your cow," he said hoarsely, "your cow, Miss Pickerell, is acting very strangely. She keeps pawing the ground and sniffing at the air and . . ."

"Animals can sense earth tremors," Professor Humwhistel told him quietly.

"I've never seen her so restless," Mr. Kettelson

49

continued. "I'm certain she's not sick, Miss Pickerell. I felt her nose immediately. It's cold as usual and her . . ."

He stopped suddenly and stared at Professor Humwhistel.

"What did you say?" he asked. "Earth WHAT?"

Miss Pickerell spoke before Professor Humwhistel had a chance to answer.

"I must go to . . . ," she began.

A dull thud from the hallway interrupted whatever else she was going to say. Euphus made a running leap to get there first.

"It's your needlepoint pillows!" he shouted to Miss Pickerell. "They fell off your horsehair sofa. Your box of talcum powder fell off your dresser in the bedroom, too."

"I gather Pumpkins is pushing things around again," Mr. Kettelson said, smiling. "He still acts like a kitten."

But Pumpkins had not moved out of the kitchen. He was sitting on the table, his ears lifted high, staring at the white kitchen cabinets.

Miss Pickerell stared, too. She was sure that the cups inside were rattling. She said so to Professor Humwhistel.

"I heard nothing," Professor Humwhistel replied, sounding more calm than he looked, while he opened a cabinet door and pointed to the cups safely hanging on their hooks. "You were imagining it, Miss Pickerell."

"Perhaps," Miss Pickerell said tersely. "But

Pumpkins wasn't. And you, yourself, Professor, remarked just a moment ago that animals can sense earth tremors."

"What earth tremors?" Mr. Kettelson demanded.

Pumpkins jumped down from the table at the precise second that Miss Pickerell's candlestick came clattering off the counter top. Miss Pickerell picked him up and held him close.

"This is it!" she declared. "There can be no more question about it."

"Question about WHAT?" Mr. Kettelson shouted.

Miss Pickerell let Pumpkins slide down to the floor.

"The earthquake, Mr. Kettelson," she said quietly. "It has struck Heatherbarrow City. And, as far as I have been able to gather from Professor Humwhistel's few words, Square Toe County is right in the earthquake line."

The Mrs. Beeton Cooking Hour blared out of the radio again. Mrs. Beeton was explaining in a very high-pitched, enthusiastic voice exactly how to rotate the cauliflower for the best browning results.

"I can assure you both," Professor Humwhistel said, as he quickly turned down the volume, "I can assure you both from personal earthquake experience that we are feeling only an earth tremor. You are overexcited, Miss Pickerell."

"Not at all," Miss Pickerell said, trying hard to forget about the butterflies in her stomach and, at the same time, to keep her voice steady. "But I am definitely not waiting until what you call a tremor becomes a quake. Where is that map you drew in the diner, Professor? I would like to borrow it, if you don't mind."

Professor Humwhistel emptied his right pocket and then proceeded to search in the left one.

"And Euphus," Miss Pickerell stated, "please let me have the outline you made in the car."

Euphus gave it to her. Miss Pickerell carefully placed it, together with the very crumpled napkin that Professor Humwhistel handed over, in her knitting bag. She then tucked her umbrella under her arm and firmly set her hat on her head. Mr. Kettelson opened his mouth wide.

"Where . . . Where . . . ?" he spluttered.

"I am going to see Professor Humwhistel's friends in their cave," Miss Pickerell answered. "What did you say their names were, Professor?"

"Dr. Donner and Dr. Blitzenkrieg," Professor Humwhistel muttered. "But I told you, Miss Pickerell. They have not answered my letters. The men have *disappeared.*"

"I will find them," Miss Pickerell said confidently.

Mr. Kettelson shook his head.

"It sounds dangerous to me," he sighed. "All those missiles and bombs that Euphus mentioned!"

"Don't leave out the spies," Euphus reminded him.

"I don't think you ought to let your imagination run away with you," Miss Pickerell told him bluntly.

She stooped to pick up Pumpkins, who was now crouched under a chair.

"Mr. Kettelson," she asked, "will you please bring my cow from the pasture? It will save time."

Mr. Kettelson opened his mouth still wider and made an effort to find his voice.

"Surely, Miss Pickerell," he said finally, "surely, you will not take your animals with you. You may well have all you can do to protect yourself."

"Certainly my animals go with me," Miss

Pickerell said sternly. "You do not think for one moment, do you, Mr. Kettelson, that I would leave them behind when there is even a suggestion of an earthquake? They go with me where I can keep an eye on them. And I am telephoning your parents to come and take you home, Euphus. I am not taking any chances."

"Not much," Mr. Kettelson snorted half under his breath. "Not much!"

5

IN THE MIDDLE
OF NOWHERE

When Nancy Agatha was back in her trailer and Pumpkins settled in the spot he had chosen, across the top of the driver's seat, Mr. Kettelson stepped into the automobile.

"I'm going with you, Miss Pickerell," he said sadly. "I really don't care for this kind of journey at all. But I feel it is my duty. You never know, Miss Pickerell, when you'll have to leave your animals alone while you're hunting around for those irresponsible scientists. I couldn't . . ."

"Mr. Kettelson—" Miss Pickerell tried to interrupt.

"I couldn't bear it," Mr. Kettelson finished,

"if anything happened to Nancy Agatha or to Pumpkins, while you were away from them."

Miss Pickerell frowned. Mr. Kettelson should certainly know that she would be the *last* person to leave her animals alone in such circumstances! But she did not want to take the time to argue.

"Very well," she said, moving over and making room for him. "Provided you don't talk. I have a lot to think about."

Mr. Kettelson nodded silently.

"I want to review in my mind the earthquake causes so that I can discuss them fully with Dr. Donner and Dr. Blitzenkrieg," she added.

Mr. Kettelson nodded again.

Miss Pickerell briskly steered the car down the private lane and onto the main road that led to the highway. She did not slow down to say "Good afternoon" to the two attendants in the garage near the end of the lane when they waved and called, "Hi, Miss Pickerell! Hi, Nancy Agatha and Pumpkins!" She drove steadily on. Mr. Kettelson looked at her hesitantly.

"If . . . ," he stammered, "If . . ."

"Yes, Mr. Kettelson?" Miss Pickerell inquired. "What is it you want to say?"

"If I may ask one question . . . ," he ventured.

"Only one," Miss Pickerell agreed.

"Just . . . just how do you intend to find that cave?" he asked, whispering.

"You needn't whisper, Mr. Kettelson," Miss Pickerell told him. "The answer is simple. I will follow Euphus's dots."

"Those dots seemed pretty vague to me," Mr. Kettelson mumbled.

"They were perfectly clear to *me*," Miss Pickerell replied stiffly.

"And then," Mr. Kettelson went on, "when you find the cave . . ."

"Mr. Kettelson," Miss Pickerell interrupted, "I don't mean to be impolite, but you are asking me *two* questions and . . ."

"Yes, yes," Mr. Kettelson said quickly.

They descended the mountain and entered Square Toe City in absolute silence. Miss Pickerell avoided the busy streets and drove along the quiet avenues where the traffic was lighter. They passed the school, closed for the summer, the police station with the two green lamps in front of it, and the new yarn store where the three ladies from the Why Not Knit It Department of Square Toe City's General Store had set themselves up in a business of their own. All three ladies were sitting on camp stools in front of the store.

"Business does not seem to be too good for them," Miss Pickerell observed.

"Business, these days," Mr. Kettelson replied glumly, "is not too good for anybody. I am seriously thinking of closing down my hardware store altogether."

Miss Pickerell smiled. Mr. Kettelson had been saying that for years.

She drove on, past the railroad depot and the typewriter company and the chocolate factory right near the typewriter company and the motel on the other side of the chocolate factory and made a sharp turn to the left.

"This, I believe," she said, "is where we begin climbing toward the bypass. Mr. Kettelson, please be so kind as to consult a map to make sure. There are a number of local maps in the glove compartment. The one we need is right on top."

Mr. Kettelson took out the map and unfolded it.

"I . . . I'm afraid I don't read maps very well," he said.

"We'll both look at it," Miss Pickerell said,

pulling off the road and coming to a halt.

She took a pencil out of her knitting bag and drew a long, dark line straight up from Square Toe City.

"This," she said, when she stopped, "is about where Professor Humwhistel said the bypass begins. We'll find that first. Then, we'll follow the professor's and Euphus's dots."

Mr. Kettelson looked grimmer than ever when she began to drive again. Miss Pickerell half wished that it was Mr. Rugby, instead of Mr. Kettelson, who was riding with her. Mr.

Rugby was always so jolly. Of course, he would have insisted on taking one of his shortcuts and they would have gotten lost. Miss Pickerell laughed to herself thinking about Mr. Rugby's shortcuts.

They were leaving the outskirts of the city now. The homes and the shops grew farther and farther apart. Farms and weatherbeaten barns and wire chicken houses took their place. After a few miles, these too disappeared. There was nothing but the road ahead and thick, towering trees on either side. Their branches brushed against the top of the car when the road narrowed. Once, Miss Pickerell stopped to make sure that her cow was all right. Another time, when the branches seemed almost to be pushing their way through the windows, Pumpkins gave out a loud meow.

Then, suddenly it began to rain. The drops spattered against the windshield and the car windows and on the awning over the trailer. The road, banked on either side with sodden leaves, started to wind. Miss Pickerell kept her hands tightly on the wheel and drove resolutely on. She slowed down only when she made the turn at the bypass.

"Now we're on our way," she said.

They were entering farmland again. Miss Pickerell relaxed when she saw the fields ahead. But she stiffened abruptly when she drove by them and took a closer look. The top soil was jaggedly ripped. The grass everywhere was scarred. The stunted bushes seemed to be gasping for air. And the houses and the barns and the chicken coops were all abandoned and shut tight. Miss Pickerell shivered. Mr. Kettelson, squirming in the seat beside her, was certainly no help. She could almost sense his fear.

"It looks like the end of the world to me," he said between clenched teeth.

"Not at all," Miss Pickerell replied.

She hoped that she sounded braver than she felt. They had been traveling for only two hours. It seemed more like two days. Everything that was happening was so unexpected—the deserted countryside, the scarred land, even the behavior of the automobile. The engine was hissing and rattling and making banging sounds she had never heard before.

"It's going to explode," Mr. Kettelson said flatly.

"Not my automobile! Not . . . ," Miss Pickerell started to protest.

She stopped when more clunking noises came

from inside the car. Then the motor gave out a dreadful sputter, the automobile shook from side to side, and, after one last violent bounce, went absolutely dead.

Mr. Kettelson's face turned ashen gray. He leaned forward as if he had a bellyache.

"Miss Pickerell," he said, when he straightened himself up again, "if you will just look at your gas gauge, you will see that . . ."

Miss Pickerell looked. The arrow pointed to zero. The car couldn't possibly move. There was not a drop of gas left in the tank.

"We are stuck," she whispered, trying hard to control her panic.

"In the middle of nowhere," Mr. Kettelson whispered back.

6

INSIDE THE GATES

"Not really!" Miss Pickerell said suddenly.

"I beg your pardon," Mr. Kettelson asked, staring at her.

"We are not really in the middle of nowhere, Mr. Kettelson," Miss Pickerell explained. "I can see clearly that there is an abandoned gas station up ahead. Now, if they left any gas in their . . ."

She did not take the time to finish her sentence. She paused only to pat Pumpkins and Nancy Agatha on the head and to tell them she would be right back. She quickly reached for the large emergency can, lying together with a rusty wrench and a double battery-powered searchlight under the back seat of the car. Slanting her umbrella against the rain, she raced up the road to the gas station. Mr. Kettelson ran after her.

"There will be enough to fill this can," she said, after she made her inspection and began to pump happily.

"And then? Then what?" Mr. Kettelson wanted to know.

"It is a sizable can," Miss Pickerell answered. "We will be able to go a long way with what we have."

"How long?" Mr. Kettelson muttered.

Miss Pickerell did not reply. She was debating with herself about whether or not to pay for the gas. There was no one to whom she could give the money. But she did not feel that it was quite honest to go off without paying.

"I think I'll just leave the money in that little office up there," she said to herself. "And if there is a piece of paper around, I'll also leave a note."

The door to the office was open. Whoever had been there must have left in a dreadful hurry, for the radio on the brown wooden desk was still on.

"The water in Heatherbarrow City," a voice was saying, "is rising. It has gone up half an inch since the earthquake erupted. The earthquake registered between 3.3 and 3.9 on the Richter scale. This can still be considered a minor quake. But, according to current evidence, a big one, measuring perhaps 6.1 or 6.2, could follow within forty-eight hours or less. Evacuation from Heatherbarrow City is proceeding in an orderly fashion. The Police and Fire Departments are . . ."

Miss Pickerell did not know that she had any right to do so but she turned the radio off. She was glad that Mr. Kettelson had not joined her in the office. He would confuse her altogether with his nervousness. Not that she felt any less so, she had to admit. But she had no intention of giving into the feeling.

She carefully figured out what she believed was the right amount for the gas and put it in the middle of the desk. She explained this in the note she wrote on the owner's memo pad, and left her name and telephone number, in case her figuring was not correct. She mentioned, too, her opinion of the price of gas these days.

Mr. Kettelson had gone back to the car. She could see him pouring the gas from the can into the tank in the rear of the automobile.

"Thank you, Mr. Kettelson," she said, as they settled themselves in the front seat again. "We can drive on now."

They drove on under dripping tunnels formed by the twisted boughs of trees. The rain had stopped. But the winds gusted all around them. The car swayed from side to side. Mr. Kettelson noticed it immediately.

"Did you feel *that*, Miss Pickerell?" he asked.

"It's the wind," Miss Pickerell said, trying to reassure herself, as well as Mr. Kettelson.

"It could be another tremor," Mr. Kettelson insisted.

Miss Pickerell did not answer. She was concentrating on her driving. The wheel was becoming more and more difficult to control. And the roof of the car made squeaking noises, as though it was getting ready to fly off.

"We are in earthquake country," Mr. Kettelson said, whispering again.

"Look!" Miss Pickerell excitedly burst out. "Look, Mr. Kettelson!"

"If you mean in the direction of Heatherbarrow City," Mr. Kettelson replied, "I see no point in doing so. I am feeling desperate enough, as it is. And, any minute now, we, too, may be . . ."

"Look!" Miss Pickerell said once more, this time pointing down the hillside they were descending.

A huge hole, shaped like an upside-down U, was clearly visible in the opposite hillside. Mr. Kettelson stopped talking to stare at it.

"The cave!" Miss Pickerell whispered, staring too and observing that a dark gray building, almost hidden by the trees, flanked it on one side.

"Spies!" Mr. Kettelson hissed. "Spies, hiding out in the wilderness! With bombs and missiles and goodness knows what else!"

Whoever and whatever lurked in the cave and in the gray shadowy building, Miss Pickerell

certainly didn't think it was spies. That was nonsense.

"Oh, pooh!" she said impatiently.

"Pooh, nothing!" Mr. Kettelson retorted. "If those two doctor scientists have really been studying so hard and so long, why haven't they done something to prevent this terrible thing that is happening in Heatherbarrow City

and, for all we know, right this minute in
Square . . ."

Miss Pickerell felt her heart sink to her toes.
She couldn't bear to listen to him anymore.

"That's what I intend to find out," she interrupted, firmly pulling herself together and driving resolutely on. "I'm marching right into that
building and I'm asking some questions!"

Getting inside, however, was not going to be easy. She realized this as the car drew nearer and she saw the heavy, iron fence. It stretched in seemingly endless fashion before her and stood, Miss Pickerell calculated, about three times as tall as she did. Enormous white signs posted on it to the right and left announced in giant red letters that this was an electric fence with HIGH VOLTAGE. Even heavier letters, above and beneath the announcement, spelled out the word DANGER. Miss Pickerell shivered. But she kept on driving until they were only a few feet away from the fence. Then she jolted the car to a sharp stop, made certain her hat was on straight, and picked up her knitting bag and her umbrella.

"What now?" Mr. Kettelson breathed.

Miss Pickerell pointed again, this time to a massive iron gate in the middle of the fence.

"I'm going in," she announced, stepping briskly out of the car.

Mr. Kettelson, wringing his hands, sat rooted to his seat. He moved only to grab Pumpkins, who was getting ready to leap out, too, and follow Miss Pickerell.

"I'll stay with the animals," he said mournfully.

Miss Pickerell nodded silently. She paused only to restraighten her hat. Then she walked slowly toward the bell that hung on a chain at the right side of the gate. She would have liked to have moved more quickly and get it over with but the wind was too strong. Twice she had to lean on her closed umbrella to keep from being blown over. And once, right near the gate, an especially strong gust forced her to cling to a tree for support.

The clanging of the bell mixed itself up with the howling of the wind when Miss Pickerell pulled on the chain. The massive gate swung open even before she had a chance to take her hand away. She stepped quickly inside. It was not a moment too soon. She had barely pulled her umbrella and her second foot in when the gate clanged shut behind her.

"Forevermore!" she whispered, as she peered over her clouded glasses for a better look and listened carefully to what was happening.

7

MISS PICKERELL WAITS

A second, smaller gate attached to an inner fence was slowly being opened by a key that Miss Pickerell could see turning in the rusty lock. The gate creaked heavily as it opened outward. A tall young man with huge, dark-framed glasses that made him look like an owl emerged. He had round cheeks and freckles and was wearing a walkie-talkie around his neck and an orange-colored construction worker's helmet on his head. He reminded Miss Pickerell of her oldest nephew, Dwight, who also wore a helmet whenever Professor Humwhistel let him borrow his motorcycle.

"Your lock needs oiling," Miss Pickerell commented. "So does your gate."

The young man smiled hesitantly and politely raised his helmet.

"Yes?" he asked. "What can I do for you?"

"I'm Miss Pickerell from Square Toe Farm," Miss Pickerell replied crisply. "I'm looking for Dr. Donner and Dr. Blitzenkrieg. Are they here?"

The young man seemed to stiffen.

"I'm not supposed to say," he answered.

Miss Pickerell had all she could do to keep from exploding.

"Look here, Mr. Whatever Your Name Is . . . ," she began.

"I'm Reuben Read," the young man told her, "Junior Assistant Reuben Read."

"Look here, Mr. Reuben Read," Miss Pickerell continued, practically spitting out her words, "an earthquake is raging up and down this countryside and you have the colossal nerve to stand there and . . ."

"We know about the earthquake," Mr. Read said, when she paused to take a breath. "We are studying its progress on our seismographs in the blueprint room."

"The blueprint room!" Miss Pickerell exclaimed, almost beside herself with outrage. "*Studying* an earthquake in the blueprint room! Why don't you go out and *see* what is happening?"

"We *know* what is happening," Mr. Read replied stubbornly.

Miss Pickerell gave a brief "Humph."

"I can prove it," Mr. Read said, just as shortly.

He consulted a piece of paper that he had been holding in his left hand. He proceeded immediately to read from it.

"Just one minute ago," he recited, pronouncing every word very distinctly, "a trench across a fault near Heatherbarrow City collapsed. A number of bricks have fallen out of some of the larger buildings in that vicinity. Two cars have skidded off a bridge. Three telephone poles have split apart. Our probability curves indicate that a major earthquake may occur in . . ."

"In forty-eight hours," Miss Pickerell broke in. "Or less! I know all that. What I *don't* know, as I began to say before, is how you can stand there, Mr. Reuben Read, and refuse to let me talk to Dr. Donner and Dr. Blitzenkrieg, who are supposed to be specialists in earthquake prevention. What *are* they doing here, anyhow?"

Mr. Read turned red.

"It's . . . It's a secret," he said, stammering a little.

"A secret!" Miss Pickerell gasped. "At a time like this? Why, that's the most ridiculous nonsense I ever heard!"

She resolutely started to walk through the gate. Mr. Read stepped in front of her and barred the way.

"May I . . . ," Miss Pickerell asked, thinking fast, "may I use your telephone? I would like to call the Governor."

Mr. Read blinked at her uncertainly through his glasses.

"I really would like to give you permission, Miss Pickerell," he replied. "But I don't have the authority."

"Somebody must have the authority," Miss Pickerell insisted.

Mr. Read removed his helmet and scratched his head.

"I suppose," he said thoughtfully, "I suppose I can get a message through to my chief about that."

He looked up at the heavily clouded sky and at Miss Pickerell leaning against the gate in the wind.

"And I guess," he added, "I can take you as far as the waiting room. Please follow me, Miss Pickerell."

He led the way up and then down a zig-zagging gravel path, past the cave entrance, and along the side of the dark gray building. Miss Pickerell noticed that an overpass connected the top of the cave with the building. She wondered whether there wasn't an underpass as well.

They moved on to another path, this one very narrow and paved with cobblestones. Grass grew on either side. It was mostly scarred grass, though. Except for one blob of chrysanthemums and a few green aspidistra leaves bravely pushing themselves up through the soil, there were no flowers. The trees, Miss Pickerell was sorry to see, were in an even worse condition than the bushes she had observed from her automobile.

"Mr. Read," she said, just before he made a turn to the back of the building and glanced around to make sure that she was right behind him, "the vegetation here puzzles me. At this time of year, the trees should still be thick with leaves and the . . ."

Mr. Read stopped short suddenly.

"Miss Pickerell," he said firmly, "I'm *not* supposed to answer such important questions. And if you keep on asking them, I will have to escort you back outside the gates."

Miss Pickerell dismissed the idea with a vigorous wave of her umbrella.

"I don't see that it is such an important question," she retorted. "The condition can probably be resolved very simply with some good fertilizer. Now, on my farm, I never fail to . . ."

"Miss Pickerell," Mr. Read interrupted, "I think . . . I think maybe I should not let you in, after all."

"Not let me into the waiting room?" Miss Pickerell exclaimed, her voice quivering with indignation. "Because I strongly believe in the regular use of fertilizer on the land? Well, I never! If this isn't the silliest . . ."

Mr. Read shook his head helplessly and resumed walking. They passed door after door, all bordering on the cobblestone path. Each door was marked with a consecutive letter of the alphabet. Miss Pickerell wished it wasn't so far to the letter W, which would, she supposed, stand for WAITING ROOM. Her feet were beginning to hurt. Running after Mr. Read on the rough cobblestones was no picnic. She slowed down after the letter S to catch her breath. Mr. Read paused in front of the next door. It had no letter on it.

"Here we are," he said, pushing the door open and holding it ajar while she entered.

"How long will I have to wait?" Miss Pickerell asked immediately.

Mr. Read did not answer. He carefully adjusted the spring lock on the door. He left her, after sharply snapping the door shut and testing it twice to make certain that it could definitely not be opened.

8

MISS PICKERELL
PUSHES THE BUTTON

"Nonsense!" Miss Pickerell said, the minute his footsteps could no longer be heard. "Snaplocks cannot be opened from the outside without a key. But they can certainly be opened from the inside."

This door, however, could not be opened from the inside, either. No matter how many ways she turned the lock or twisted the knob, the door remained firmly shut. Miss Pickerell could not understand it at all. A small, cold chill was slowly starting to trickle down her spine.

"Nonsense!" she said again, as she tried to pull herself together. "He's a nice young man. He'll be back soon."

She decided to walk around the room to help pass the time. It was a small room, oval-shaped and windowless, that looked more like an office than a place for visitors. The heavy oak table in the center was piled high with clippings cut out of newspapers and magazines. A bulletin board on a nearby wall had six notices attached to it with white thumb tacks. Most of the notices, Miss Pickerell observed, were about dates and places of meetings. One notice, on an especially large piece of paper, announced that coffee would no longer be served if people didn't wash their cups or clean out the coffee pot.

The writer of this notice was evidently as good as his word. The pot on the small electric plate near the far end of the table was empty and so was the jar of instant coffee standing next to it. Miss Pickerell was sorry. She was cold and thirsty and would have appreciated something hot to drink.

The water cooler on the other side of the room was full, though. Miss Pickerell took a paper cup out of the container on the wall and helped herself. She was glad it was spring water. That was usually very refreshing.

She glanced at the clippings as she moved

them aside to make room for her cup on the table. Most of them were about fractures in the earth's plates and earthquake-prediction methods. The newspaper clippings were mostly easier to understand than those from the magazines. Miss Pickerell thought they really ought to be separated into two batches, with the latest dates of each on top.

"I'll have to remember to tell Mr. Reuben Read about that," she said.

She patted the clippings neatly back into place and went to throw her empty cup into the basket near the water cooler. She looked at her watch and compared it with the clock above the bulletin board. They were both the same. The hands stood at exactly twenty minutes after four.

"This is ridiculous!" she exclaimed. "It *can't* take so long to get permission to make a telephone call."

She walked over to the door and banged on it. "Yoo-hoo!" she called. "Yoo-hoo, Mr. Read!" No one answered.

"Yoo-hoo!" she called again, banging louder.

Silence, broken only by the echo of her voice, followed. Miss Pickerell stood stock-still. Visions of disappearing like Dr. Donner and Dr. Blitzenkrieg began to float through her mind.

"It's nerves!" she told herself. "Nothing but nerves! After all, there must be somebody in this building, somebody behind all those closed doors we passed."

On second thought, she wasn't so sure about that. There were some offices where everybody went home early in the summertime. She often wondered how they ever managed to get any work done.

"Well, I'll have to do something while I'm waiting," she reasoned, trying to be practical.

She sat down at the table again and opened her knitting bag. The green-and-white skirt she was crocheting for Rosemary was in there and so was a pair of socks with a diamond pattern that she was making for Euphus.

"I'll turn the heel on that second sock right now," she said. "Then it won't take too long to finish."

Her knitting needles clicked briskly as she rushed from one row to the next, pausing only to recount her stitches. But she couldn't keep her mind on the pattern. She gave up after the fourth row.

"Euphus's socks will have to wait," she said decisively. "I must get out of here."

She hurried back to the door. She banged on it with both her fists. She walked all around the room, banging on each wall and shouting "Yoohoo" at the top of her lungs. Then she climbed up on the table in the middle of the room, stood there on tip toe, and banged her umbrella against the ceiling.

"Help! Help!" she screamed, her voice by now dry and cracked.

If anyone heard her, that person made no reply.

"The whole place is probably soundproof," she told herself dully.

She couldn't remember ever having felt so dismal and hopeless before. The thoughts about Dr. Donner and Dr. Blitzenkrieg kept going around and around in her head.

"I may never see Euphus or Rosemary or Mr. Kettelson or my Nancy Agatha or Pumpkins or *anybody* again," she whispered, choking back the tears that were surging up in her throat. "And I will certainly never be able to do anything about earthquake prevention. I can't imagine whatever made me think that I might."

It was when she was getting off the table that she noticed the panel of buttons half hidden by a bookcase diagonally across from the water cooler. Every button, she saw when she walked over for a closer look, was a different color. And each one had a little printed label directly above it.

She had no idea what the labels over the pink, lavender, and yellow ones in the top row meant. And she couldn't even read the labels over the green, brown, and blue buttons in the second row.

"I suppose they were scribbled by some doctor," she decided. "Doctors have those awful handwritings."

But the label over the single red button on the bottom row was as clear as it could be. The letters were large and so were the spaces between them. Miss Pickerell spelled them out twice.

"WATERFOWL! WATERFOWL!" she recited breathlessly.

Something was stirring in her brain, some nagging recollection that made the word familiar. Euphus came into it somewhere. And Professor Humwhistel . . .

"Of course!" she suddenly exclaimed out loud. "It's the project that Dr. Donner and Dr. Blitzenkrieg are working on. And Euphus sat in the back of the trailer and said it was a crazy name for an earthquake-prevention project. It certainly is. No wonder I didn't remember it right away."

She knew exactly what she had to do now. She would press the button for those two friends of Professor Humwhistel's. And when they showed up, she would give them a good piece of her mind.

She was just breathing a deep sigh of relief when a new thought suddenly struck her. It was a very unsettling thought with two very distinct sides to it. She sat down to debate the two sides thoroughly.

"On the one hand," she argued, silently at first and then aloud so that she could examine the arguments as she went along, "on the one hand, everybody knows that wars and all sorts of terrible things can happen if a person pushes an important button that he or she should not push!"

She paused to take another deep breath.

"On the other hand," she went on, "this is not that kind of button. And it is marked WATER-FOWL. And if I don't push it, and that earth-quake, measuring 6.1 to 6.2 on the Richter scale . . ."

She couldn't stand even to think about it. She got up and walked over to the panel.

"Now if only that Mr. Reuben Read came back," she said, talking directly to the button, "I could tell him about you. And I could *demand* to see Dr. Donner and Dr. Blitzenkrieg."

Thinking about Mr. Read made her feel lonely and frightened again. It was almost five o'clock. Would he ever come back? Or would she just be left in that room with the clippings and the empty coffee pot and . . .

"At least, if I push the button, someone will *hear* me," she exclaimed, as she let her fingers slide up and down the panel. "And it doesn't say anywhere DO NOT TOUCH."

She reconsidered and quickly moved her fingers away.

"It must be *some* important button," she warned herself. "It's *red* and it's on a row all by itself and . . ."

She examined her watch once more. She reached out and let her right forefinger lightly touch the lone red button on the bottom of the panel.

"I must do something," she breathed. "I must! I must!"

She closed her eyes. She pushed before she had a chance to change her mind again.

And then the most unexpected thing of all happened. The wall where the panel of buttons was attached slid open. An empty elevator, made of bars and heavy chicken wire, faced her. The front section swung outward to provide a narrow entrance.

"What now?" she asked, her voice trembling.

She brushed aside the doubts that came popping, one after another, into her head. She steeled herself to *whatever* would come next. Her knitting bag dangling on one arm and her umbrella on the other, she marched through the opening and into the cagelike elevator.

9

DOWN! DOWN! DOWN!

There were no buttons to press in the elevator. It simply started to go down as soon as the front section sprang shut. Miss Pickerell concluded that she must be descending into a basement.

"Now why didn't I think of a basement?" she asked herself. "I could have banged on the floor and somebody there would probably have heard me. Oh, well!"

She felt much calmer now that there was the hope of some action. Dr. Donner and Dr. Blitzenkrieg were most likely working in the basement. After all, she had pushed the WATER-FOWL button and that was the project they were engaged in.

"And I certainly will tell them what I think of their behavior when I meet them," she said, relishing the prospect. She did not want to be rude but she definitely believed that they had a very stern lecture coming to them.

"Such utter irresponsibility!" she said out loud. "Well, I'll just have to see to it that they start to use their brains and accomplish something."

Miss Pickerell had great faith in science. She reviewed in her mind a few of the advances science had made possible: penicillin, electricity, voyages to outer space, the radio, the telephone . . . Why, two hundred years ago nobody would have believed such things could be. People would have laughed if you told them they could simply pick up a little instrument and speak to someone across thousands of miles, millions if you counted the distance to Mars or the moon. And these days, they were even talking about finding valuable minerals on the sea bottom and about how oxygen could be supplied by the sea, instead of by trees and plants. She let out a little sigh of contentment.

"Scientists who can think of all that," she said decisively, "can certainly learn how to prevent an earthquake."

The elevator slowed down and creaked slightly.

"I guess we're getting ready to stop," Miss Pickerell remarked, giving the back of her hair a little pat and holding on tight to her knitting bag and umbrella, just in case the front should spring open fast, the way the outside gate had done. "Now I have to find Dr. Donner and Dr. Blitzenkrieg."

But the elevator did not stop. The creak became a groan, the cage lurched sharply to one side, and the descent suddenly became more rapid.

Miss Pickerell shook her head. She never could understand why builders so often dug such deep basements. They were hardly ever practical. Her own basement on the farm was just deep enough to be cool in the summer so that she could keep her preserves there. And she didn't have to walk too many steps to go up or down.

She moved up to the bars and peered between them. All she could see was a dark, straight shaft that went on and on and layers of jagged rock all around. Strange yellow growths clung to the crevices in the rocks. Weird plants—or *were* they plants—hung on either side. Some of them were shaped like the cones that Mr. Rugby put his ice cream into and others like upside-down ice-cream cones.

She adjusted her glasses and took another look.

"No," she said thoughtfully, "they're more like icicles."

She leaned back in the elevator while she tried to remember what they reminded her of. For a moment, she wondered if it was a picture of some stalactites and stalagmites that she had seen on a television nature show once. She had wanted to look them up in her encyclopedia right after the show and had searched all over the house for the S volume. Then she realized that Mr. Esticott, the baggage master, had borrowed it. His daughter in Plentibush City had written to tell him that she attended a concert where all the music was very staccato. He wasn't entirely sure that he understood what she meant. Even after Miss Pickerell told him that it was the way Rosemary practiced on the piano so that the notes never even sounded as though they belonged to each other, he didn't really understand. He insisted on borrowing the S volume to study the word by himself, at home.

And he still hadn't returned it, Miss Pickerell reflected.

She thought again about the television show. The nature-study man—he was called a spelunker—had explained each picture as it appeared on the screen. He had said that the stalactites and stalagmites were part of the earth's changes. They could be found way down in the earth's hollow places where . . .

Miss Pickerell jumped. She opened her mouth to say something but no voice came out. She was staring at something new on the walls outside of the elevator and she was beginning to understand.

"Oh, no!" she gasped. "Oh, no! It can't be!"

What she saw were numbers printed in that fluorescent paint she sometimes saw down the center of highways. The bulb in the ceiling of the elevator illuminated the numbers clearly. She whispered them hoarsely to herself as she passed them: "Five thousand feet (151.17 meters); sixty-eight hundred feet (206.0 meters); seventy-two hundred feet (210.0 meters); seventy-eight hundred feet . . ." What was it that Professor Humwhistel had said when he was talking about how deep they sometimes went

down into the earth to do their experiments—
25,000 feet? Yes, she remembered exactly. He
had definitely said 25,000 feet.

"Twenty-five thousand feet!" she whispered.
"Down twenty-five thousand feet into the earth!
That's where I'm probably going!"

Her mind reeled at the very thought. And her
heart practically stood still when she reflected
that she might well be the only human being
down there.

These days, scientists did things by remote
control. Maybe they sent robot instruments
down in that elevator and some electronic TV
system beamed in on them and . . . She didn't
really know what to think. Her head was swim-
ming with dizziness.

The elevator was moving relentlessly on,
down, down to the interior of the earth. It was
also shaking and making low, moaning noises.
They sounded to Miss Pickerell like the monoto-
nous sing-song of a steam train and each moan
seemed to be saying, "25,000 feet! 25,000 feet!
25,000 feet! 25,000 feet under the ground!"

She started counting the bars on the elevator
to get the tune out of her head. But there were
only sixteen bars, and even when she counted

them three times, she had soon finished. And the elevator was still going down.

"I don't have to be so frightened," she told herself, trying desperately to be practical. "I'll find some button to push that will take me right up again. And I'll simply have to wait for that Mr. Reuben Read. It's just that I never intended to travel into the earth's interior. Not even Mr. Kettelson can say that I planned any such thing."

She was making every effort to remain cool and collected. It was getting harder and harder to do, though. And was it her imagination or was the narrow shaft growing hotter by the minute? One thing she *did* know was that she was finding it very difficult to breathe. She tried inhaling and exhaling slowly to steady herself. That didn't help much. She leaned wearily against the front of the cage, hearing again the unceasing chant, "25,000 feet! 25,000 feet! 25,000 feet under the . . ."

And then, without warning, the creaking and the moaning stopped. The elevator came to a hissing halt. The front unlatched and sprang open. And Miss Pickerell fell right into the arms of a man with a sweeping mustache and slightly

stooping shoulders. Just before everything went black, she recognized her old friend, Professor Tuttle.

10

BEHIND BARS
WITH PROFESSOR TUTTLE

When Miss Pickerell opened her eyes, she was sitting in a deep leather armchair across a desk from Professor Tuttle. He was smiling in the very cheerful way he used to when she first met him on a dig a few years ago. And he was offering her a cup of cocoa and a sandwich, both neatly arranged on a tray with a napkin, some extra sugar in a bowl, and a deeper bowl with whipped cream in it.

"Now don't apologize for fainting, Miss Pickerell," he said briskly. "Everybody feels limp the first time they come down that ghostly elevator. In part, it's because they haven't installed any air-conditioning there as yet. Here, of course, the air is comfortably controlled."

He pushed the tray closer.

"I hope you like your cocoa strong," he continued. "My secretary, Ernestine, is a firm believer in strong cocoa. She considers it an excellent tonic for the nerves."

Miss Pickerell glanced around her in dazed bewilderment. She could find no digging anywhere she looked. She could see only desks and chairs and filing cabinets and men and women busily working at typewriters and drawing boards and calculators and mostly at computers. It was a very big office.

"I . . . I thought I was going twenty-five thousand feet underground," she stammered, shivering a little with the memory.

"Oh, no," Professor Tuttle said, getting the point immediately. "We're not working that deep here. Not yet, anyway. It's something quite different. Quite, quite different!"

Miss Pickerell looked at him questioningly.

Professor Tuttle did not explain. He only laughed and said, "Miss Pickerell, you are precisely ninety-one hundred feet, or approximately two hundred and fifteen meters, beneath the surface of the earth at this moment. I suppose you think that's far enough. We have our offices on this level."

Miss Pickerell seriously wondered whether

she wasn't dreaming all of this up. She stared at Professor Tuttle, at the bright eyes and the ruddy cheeks and the mustache which had been short and gray but was now long and silky and had more black in it than gray. She speculated for a moment about the possibility that Professor Tuttle dyed his mustache. But she pushed this idle question out of her head. She had more serious things to think about.

"Professor Tuttle," she spluttered weakly, "*what* are you doing here?"

"I could ask you the same question, Miss Pickerell," Professor Tuttle replied quickly. "What in the world are *you* doing here?"

Miss Pickerell tried unsuccessfully to put into the right words everything about Professor Humwhistel and his two friends, Dr. Donner and Dr. Blitzenkrieg, and the way they weren't doing their job and . . .

"I . . . I came about the earthquake," she said finally, summing it up somehow.

"Ah!" Professor Tuttle remarked.

"What I mean," Miss Pickerell went on, hoping to make her explanation a little clearer, "is that I came to see what Dr. Donner and Dr. Blitzenkrieg are doing about earthquake prevention. They are seismologists, I understand.

But you . . . you are an archeologist. Have you changed professions, Professor Tuttle?"

"Not at all," Professor Tuttle replied. "The research here is not limited to seismology."

"No?" Miss Pickerell questioned.

Professor Tuttle paused and cast a few furtive glances around him.

"I'm not entirely certain whether I ought to tell you this, Miss Pickerell," he said, leaning toward her and speaking in a very low voice, "but this cave you are in now started out as . . ."

"Am I in a cave?" Miss Pickerell interrupted. "I . . . I wasn't sure."

"Of course, you are in a cave, Miss Pickerell," Professor Tuttle told her. "When the elevator you rode in started to lurch, it was moving horizontally through an underpass from the main building into the cave. But, as I was saying, this cave you are in now started out as an experimental and highly secret missile base. Then . . ."

"That explains it," Miss Pickerell burst out, remembering the ripped top soil and the charred grass and all those stunted bushes. Radioactive fallout from missile experimentation would naturally destroy vegetation.

"I beg your pardon," Professor Tuttle asked.

"Nothing," Miss Pickerell replied. "Do go on, Professor."

"Well," Professor Tuttle resumed, "then it was decided to give up the missile site. Some of the equipment is still here. That is naturally secret, too, Miss Pickerell. Another . . ."

"That accounts for the chrysanthemums and the aspidistra leaves coming up on the side of the path," Miss Pickerell murmured. "When the missile experimentation stopped, things began growing again. And it explains why Mr. Reuben Read couldn't *talk.*"

"I don't exactly follow you, Miss Pickerell," Professor Tuttle commented a little irritably.

"Never mind," Miss Pickerell told him. "You were saying that another . . ."

"Yes," Professor Tuttle went on. "Another project took its place, a most interesting project to do with the extraction of energy from water. The water must first pass through molten rock. My knowledge of rocks as an archeologist led me to the development of this interesting discovery, which is also, by the way, still secret. The water is . . ."

Miss Pickerell, who couldn't care less at the

moment about all these secrets, was growing more and more impatient.

"What about earthquake prevention, Professor Tuttle?" she cut in.

"Yes, yes, earthquake prevention," Professor Tuttle, looking startled, answered at once. "These recent occurrences have been most unfortunate. They seem to be coming at closer and closer intervals."

"They certainly do!" Miss Pickerell said acidly.

"And a number of our neighbors, I understand," Professor Tuttle went on, "have fled out of fear. My secretary, who went to have the oil in her car checked, found the gas station deserted. She was very surprised."

"I know about that gas station," Miss Pickerell snapped. "I'm asking you about earthquake prevention, Professor."

Professor Tuttle sighed heavily.

"The study of earthquake prevention is in its infancy, Miss Pickerell," he replied. "Dr. Donner and Dr. Blitzenkrieg have been working day and night on the problem. I'm not at all sure that they are nearer any solution, however."

Miss Pickerell stared, unbelieving.

"But to go on with the energy project. As I mentioned, I've made some contributions," Professor Tuttle said, paying no attention. "We begin by digging a ninety-six-hundred-foot hole through which we pump water down to the rocks. This water is retrieved through a ten-thousand-foot hole after it has percolated through the cracks. The rock-heated water has energy, Miss Pickerell, energy that can replace the oil we now so desperately need. I also have a few ideas about extracting energy from the sun. In that case, we start out by . . ."

Miss Pickerell simply could not listen anymore. She was so angry, she was nearly fit to be tied.

"Professor Tuttle," she exclaimed, shouting to drown out his voice, "what I came here about was earthquake prevention. I don't want to hear about the missiles and the energy from volcanically heated water and the energy from . . ."

She stopped, her sentence hanging in mid-air, and turned. Mr. Reuben Read, his complexion a ghastly white, was standing right behind her.

"Miss Pickerell," he asked, his voice very agitated, "how *could* you?"

"How could I what?" Miss Pickerell asked

instantly. "Escape from that silly room where you kept me waiting forever? I must say that if it takes someone in this institution so long to get permission for a single telephone call, then the institution is badly in need of reorganization. And I assure you that when I *do* make that call to the Governor, I will discuss my recommendations for reorganization thoroughly with him."

Mr. Read looked at her stonily.

"Follow me, Miss Pickerell," he said. "You too, Professor Tuttle."

"Follow you where?" Professor Tuttle demanded.

Mr. Read thrust out his jaw.

"Until I can clear this with the chief," he replied, "I am putting you in detention with Miss Pickerell. You were disclosing secret information to her."

His face went from chalk white to beet red while he talked to Professor Tuttle.

"Everybody heard you," he added apologetically.

"Nonsense!" Miss Pickerell exclaimed. "I don't know who your *chief* is. But I do know you have no right to . . ."

But when she saw Professor Tuttle rise meekly from his chair and follow Mr. Read, she did the same. She walked with them across the length of the room, down two deserted corridors, around the corner, up three darker, much narrower corridors, also deserted, and into a room that, like the elevator, had bars all around it. Only this one definitely looked more like a prison cell. Actually, Miss Pickerell realized with a sudden gasp of terror, it *was* a prison cell.

11

"IT'S TOO LATE!"

Miss Pickerell was absolutely livid with indignation. She lost no time in expressing her feelings to Professor Tuttle.

"My middle nephew, Euphus," she said, thumping on the floor with her umbrella to emphasize her words, "my middle nephew, Euphus, who watches altogether too much television, warned me about *finding* spies here. But that *I* should be *taken* for a spy!! That is about the most absurd, the most insane, the most. . ."

She stopped for a second to catch her breath.

"Why the next thing I know," she went on, "they'll be coming in here searching me for concealed weapons and turning the inside of my pockets out for secret documents and tape recording every word I . . ."

Professor Tuttle burst out laughing.

"Are you sure, Miss Pickerell," he asked, "that you don't watch even more television than Euphus?"

Miss Pickerell gave him a shocked look.

"I don't see that this is anything to joke about," she said coldly.

"It's nothing to worry about either," Professor Tuttle replied. "I can assure you, Miss Pickerell, that it will all be cleared up. Personally, I intend to use the time I spend here to complete some calculations I was working on. It is an excellent opportunity."

Miss Pickerell wanted very much to tell him that he must be out of his mind. But she decided that it would be too impolite.

"I'm afraid I have no calculations of my own to work on," she replied curtly.

"Then I suggest you catch up with your knitting," Professor Tuttle said with equal sharpness. He settled himself on one of the two stools in the room, took a thick memo pad and a pen out of his pocket, and proceeded to make very rapid notations. Miss Pickerell recognized that he was in no mood for further discussion.

She sat down on the other stool, next to Professor Tuttle, and stared unseeingly ahead of her. What was Pumpkins doing now, she wondered. And her lovely, gentle Nancy Agatha? Probably staying as close as they could to Mr. Kettelson and asking, in their own way, where she, Miss Pickerell, was all this time. That is, if there was no earthquake. Down in this terrible cave, 9,100 feet below the surface of the earth, it was impossible to know. If there *was* an earthquake . . .

Miss Pickerell got up. She simply couldn't sit still and think about it. She paced back and forth, first across the cell and then around and around it. She started at the right-hand corner, where a wash basin stood with a roll of paper towels on it, moved on to the corner at the other end, where the professor sat, huddled over his memo pad, and crossed diagonally to the corner where a cracked mirror hung near a dusty calendar. The calendar, she noticed, was turned to last-month's page. She was just putting the right page on top when she heard the swooshing of water. Swooshing? It sounded more like a torrent. No, that was not correct either. It was as though whole oceans of water were roaring somewhere to the left of her!!

"Professor Tuttle!" she cried, not caring anymore about his moods. "Do you hear what I hear?"

"Yes," he replied, without lifting his head. "The pump for pouring the water down to the rocks is very near here. It is probably being turned up to HIGH."

"High?" Miss Pickerell repeated, her mind in a muddle. She hurried back to her stool and took out Euphus's list again. There it was, in his large, childish handwriting:

④ Too much or too little lubricant.

⑤ Too much water.

④ That's easy — take some away or add just a little.

⑤ But the newspaper artical said to pump the water in ?!?>

And she remembered distinctly Professor Humwhistel saying that loading the crust with too much water could cause an earthquake. Those were almost his exact words. But she remembered, too, about the newspaper article which Professor Humwhistel had explained when they were riding from the bowling alley to Mr. Rugby's diner. The article had said to pump water along the earthquake belt. Scientists, Miss Pickerell decided, could be very confusing at times. Even Euphus hadn't completely understood this water part.

"Well," she said to herself firmly, "I'll just have to figure it out for myself."

She walked over to the front of the cell and gazed out into the narrow corridor. Mr. Reuben Read was fiddling with a dial on the wall opposite the cell. He knew she was watching him. She was sure of it when she saw him bend even lower over the dial. He lifted his head, though, when he saw a pretty girl, carrying a tray full of cups and a pitcher, coming his way. The girl walked past him and up to Miss Pickerell.

"I'm Ernestine," she said. "I have special permission to bring more cocoa. I brought some extra hot water too, in case you want to make the cocoa a little weaker."

Professor Tuttle said, "No, thank you."

Miss Pickerell, accepting only to be polite, took the cup and the pitcher that Ernestine was sliding through the bars. She promptly got rid of both the cocoa and the hot water in the basin and rinsed the cup carefully.

It was while she was pouring the water down

the basin that something began to rattle around in her brain. "A little weaker! A little weaker!" she kept thinking, because the words had started the rattling. And then, suddenly, she knew what it was. Professor Humwhistel and the newspaper article were both right. Water needed to be pumped into the ground to relieve the pressure *slowly*. That would result in harmless tremors, as Professor Humwhistel had said. But *too much* water was another story. It would relieve *so much* pressure, *all at once*, that it could cause a major earthquake, the same way that unlocking the lid of her pressure cooker once had nearly caused an explosion. The lid had actually jumped up and drops of boiling water had spurted up into her face.

"It's just those scientific terms that mixed me up," she murmured. "If only scientific people could learn to talk in everyday language some-times!"

She paced restlessly once more around the cell and made up her mind to explain the problem fully to Professor Tuttle.

"Professor," she said, walking over to him rapidly, "you must stop pouring so much water down to those rocks instantly. I can tell you exactly why."

Professor Tuttle, lightly passing a finger over his mustache, looked up briefly.

"I do wish, Miss Pickerell," he said, "that you would stop waving that umbrella around in your excitement. I assure you that I will be glad to discuss with you whatever theories you seem to have in mind at a later time."

"At a later time," Miss Pickerell repeated, her heart sinking. Why Square Toe County could well be a mass of rubble by then!

She stared scornfully into Professor Tuttle's eyes and marched over to the front of the cell again.

"Mr. Read!" she called, "Mr. Read, I need to talk to you!"

But Mr. Read had moved away. He was standing at the farthest end of the corridor, drinking cocoa with Ernestine. If he heard her call, he was ignoring it. Miss Pickerell gazed out disconsolately.

The dial on the wall in front of her, she noticed now, had a coat of luminous paint. It shone brightly in the dim light. Miss Pickerell could see the round shape of the dial, the letters H and L to the right and left of it, and the fact that it was not flush against the wall. She thought of the dimmer in the banquet room that Mr. Rugby had recently installed in his restaurant. Mr. Kettelson had sold the dimmer to Mr. Rugby at a bargain price. There were no letters around the dimmer, but you turned it to the right to make the lights high and to the left if you wanted them low. And when the customers eating in the banquet room went home, Mr. Rugby pushed the dimmer in to turn all the power off.

"Power!" Miss Pickerell whispered hoarsely. "Why that . . . that's what Mr. Read was doing when the water began to roar. He was turning the power to HIGH. Professor Tuttle practically said so when he was telling about why there was such a roar!"

The thoughts went racing through Miss Pickerell's head, as she cast hasty glances all around her. Professor Tuttle had his eyes glued to his memo pad. Mr. Reuben Read looked as though he would never tear himself away from that cocoa-drinking Ernestine. She, Miss Pickerell, could easily slide her umbrella between the bars of the cell and reach the dial across the narrow corridor. A slow, well-balanced twist with the handle would turn the dial to LOW.

She examined her umbrella critically. No! No, the handle was much too large. But . . . But

. . . Another idea was popping into her head. She frantically opened her knitting bag. Yes, there it was, right on top, the #11 curved crochet hook on Rosemary's unfinished skirt. That was heavy enough and just the right size and shape to turn the dial and make the power go down.

"That is," Miss Pickerell added, "*if* the dial is really the connection to the waterpower."

She couldn't be certain. She couldn't be certain about anything. What was it that Professor Humwhistel had asked her over his peppermintade in Mr. Rugby's diner? "Do you think, Miss Pickerell, that you will be able to accomplish more than Dr. Donner and Dr. Blitzenkrieg?"

"No," Miss Pickerell answered him mentally. "But I must try! I *have* to try!"

She stared hard at the crochet hook. It seemed a pity to take it out and drop her stitches. But really, a hairpin could easily hold the last stitch in place and then nothing would rip . . .

It took a second to catch the stitch with one of her big black hairpins and another second to thrust the hook between two of the middle bars. She reached the dial easily, curved the crochet hook firmly around it, and turned it slowly and carefully to the left.

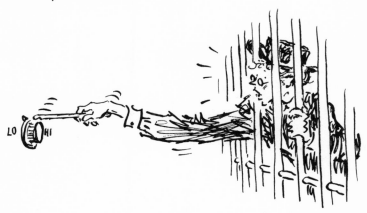

Professor Tuttle, instantly alert, screamed, "Stop! Stop!"

Mr. Reuben Read and Ernestine, both flying toward the dial, screamed back, "It's too late!" "It's too late!"

12

THE GOVERNOR WILL NEVER FORGET

"Too late for what?" Miss Pickerell demanded, as she noted the stark terror in Professor Tuttle's eyes and the frantic expression on Mr. Reuben Read's face.

A sudden beep sounded on the walkie-talkie. Mr. Reuben Read turned away from the dial and, with a trembling hand, lifted the receiver to his mouth.

"Yes, sir?" He shifted the receiver to his ear, listened a moment, then answered: "Yes, sir. I . . . I understand, sir. Right away, sir. No, I still haven't checked that out. I'll find out immediately. Yes, sir!"

The instant he clicked off the walkie-talkie, he was at the cell door.

"Miss Pickerell," he shouted, "What did you do to that dial?"

Miss Pickerell, holding out her crochet hook, stepped forward.

"I turned it to the left, Mr. Read. I turned it with this #11 hook that I use when I work with very heavy wool. It was strong enough for me to . . ."

A loud beep-beep cut her short. Mr. Read lifted the walkie-talkie again and listened intently. When he spoke, his voice shook.

"I understand fully, sir," he said. "Yes, I am making progress at this end . . . I believe it is a Miss Pickerell from Square Toe Farm . . . I will bring her up to see you . . . On the double, sir."

"Ohhh—" A sudden sob broke from Ernestine. "Oh, Miss Pickerell, he'll blame Reuben for all this," she cried, removing a handkerchief from her pocket. "You'll see. He'll say it was his fault that you . . ."

"Who is *he?*" Miss Pickerell wanted to know. "And what will he blame Mr. Reuben Read for?"

"He's the *chief,*" Ernestine wailed, through her handkerchief this time.

"And what he'll blame Mr. Read for," Professor Tuttle, pacing up and down now, shouted at her, "is for not watching you more carefully. You should have been using that crochet hook for crocheting, Miss Pickerell, instead of for turning a dial that may well have set off a major earthquake. The reports are not yet . . ."

Another beep-beep sounded on the walkie-talkie.

"Yes?" Mr. Reuben Read asked.

Miss Pickerell could make out the voice at the end quite clearly.

"There's a gentleman at the front gate," it said. "He wants to come in and see Miss Pickerell. He and Nancy Agatha and . . . I believe he said Pumpkins."

"Nancy Agatha! Pumpkins!" Mr. Read repeated, talking now to Miss Pickerell. "Who are these people?"

"Well," Miss Pickerell said, hesitating a little, "they're not *exactly* people. Nancy Agatha is my cow. And Pumpkins is my cat. They think they're people, of course, and I have never told them that they're not."

Mr. Reuben Read seemed to be trying to say something. His mouth was open. Miss Pickerell waited politely. But no words came.

"I suppose," Miss Pickerell went on, deciding that he was not going to say anything after all,

"I suppose Mr. Kettelson got tired of waiting. I can hardly blame him."

Mr. Read found some words at last.

"Miss Pickerell," he said, his face grim and chalk-white as he inserted a long, thin key into the cell door, "you and I and Professor Tuttle are going upstairs to the Communications Center to see the Chief. We are going without another word from you."

He led the way along the corridor, Ernestine at his side and Miss Pickerell and Professor Tuttle close behind him. Two men in khaki work clothes, the first one gray-haired and sad-looking, the second younger and a little plump, ran up to them on the way.

"I'm Dr. Donner," the gray-haired one whispered to Miss Pickerell.

"I'm Dr. Blitzenkrieg," the plump one whispered, too. "It's an honor for us to meet you."

Miss Pickerell had no idea why they should be honored to meet her. At this point she could think only of how much she wanted to tell them about their bad manners. But this was hardly the time or the place. She could hardly breathe, trying to keep up with Mr. Reuben Read's long strides.

"I *know* I didn't start any major earthquake,"

she said to Dr. Donner and Dr. Blitzenkrieg, who were now walking one on each side of her, Professor Tuttle having moved on ahead. "I couldn't have because I turned the dial *slowly* to LOW. I remembered about the explosion in my pressure cooker."

"A very good comparison," Dr. Donner agreed, nodding.

"A sticky bureau drawer is an even better

comparison," Dr. Blitzenkrieg commented.
"When . . ."

He paused to help Miss Pickerell walk a little
faster toward an elevator in front of them. It was
very large, with mirrors on the walls and doors
with rubber edges that rolled open and shut.
One of the doors nearly pinched Miss Pickerell,
who was the last one to get in.

"About the bureau drawer . . . ," she reminded Dr. Blitzenkrieg, once she was safely inside.

"Oh, yes," Dr. Blitzenkrieg replied. "I was going to say that when one applies a bit of oil, a sticky bureau drawer will move out quite steadily."

"Sometimes the drawer jerks a little," Miss Pickerell said, thinking about it.

"Just as the earth shakes a little with the tremors," Dr. Donner commented.

"I know exactly what you mean," Miss Pickerell told him. "Water can relieve the pressure on the earth's crust as the oil does in the bureau drawer. But a large amount will cause *internal* earth pressure that can really bring on a major earthquake the way too much oil will make the bureau drawer fly out and almost make you fly with it. And the small amount means . . ."

"Tremors only," Dr. Blitzenkrieg said helpfully.

"How often I have wanted to turn that dial down!" Dr. Donner sighed.

"Then why didn't you?" Miss Pickerell began. "You had a responsibility to . . ."

"I suggest, Miss Pickerell," Mr. Read broke in, as the elevator slid to a stop, "that you save your questions and ideas for Captain Crabapple, our chief."

With Ernestine right next to him, he stormed out. Miss Pickerell, Professor Tuttle, Dr. Donner, and Dr. Blitzenkrieg followed them along a red-carpeted corridor and into an office with a flowered blue rug and matching wallpaper. A very thin young man with an anxious face and nervously squinting eyes rose immediately from a desk at the far end of the room and came forward to meet them.

"I'm Captain Crabapple," he said, his voice gentle and quiet. "And you're Miss Pickerell, I believe, the lady from Square Toe Farm. Will you excuse me for a few minutes, Miss Pickerell? I was just about to make a telephone call. If you will please wait here . . ."

He disappeared through a side door. Miss Pickerell looked doubtfully at Mr. Reuben Read. She simply couldn't understand why he was so frightened of this nice, polite Captain Crabapple. She wondered whether she ought to speak to him about it later. Right now, she wanted to finish her conversation with Dr. Donner.

"In my opinion, Dr. Donner," she said, as she

sat down with him and Dr. Blitzenkrieg and Professor Tuttle on a very large sofa facing the desk, "in my opinion, you had a definite responsibility to turn that dial down if you believed that it would prevent an earthquake."

"We weren't *absolutely* sure of the theory," Dr. Donner replied. "It had never been tried, you see, and . . ."

"And," Professor Tuttle interrupted, waving Dr. Donner's explanation aside, "the energy-extraction project was almost completed."

"You must remember too, Miss Pickerell," Dr. Blitzenkrieg added, "that, until very recently, there seemed to be no serious danger of earthquakes in the area."

"What about that fault across Square Toe County?" Miss Pickerell demanded. "What about that fault they're always monitoring with those . . . those . . ."

"Seismographs," said Professor Tuttle, quickly supplying the word. "Their measurements usually indicated that the earthquake activity was minimal. No immediate danger was expected, and since we were eager to move along with our energy . . ."

Miss Pickerell had no patience to listen to

anymore. Her private opinion was that Dr. Donner, Dr. Blitzenkrieg, and Professor Tuttle should have gotten together for a good, long talk instead of taking this terrible chance. What *was* happening in Square Toe County right now? They were still waiting to hear . . .

"This is ridiculous," she said, walking over to the side door and staring, first at it and then at her watch. "I'll give that young chief five minutes more. If he doesn't come out by then, I'll go in and get him."

She wandered restlessly around the room, stopping to glance at the three framed photographs on the captain's desk. The biggest was a wedding picture and the man was obviously Captain Crabapple, but his squint didn't show in the picture. The photograph in the frame with the scalloped edge was of a baby kicking his heels on a curly white rug. The baby was in the third picture too, sitting in front of a house, under a tree. Miss Pickerell thought it was a speckled laurel tree. She wondered where Captain Crabapple lived.

"Well," she said, checking her watch, "I'm going to knock on that door of his right this minute."

But the captain came through the door before she got there.

"The reports that have come in are from very excited people," he said. "I've been trying to reach the Governor to give him the actual facts that have been recorded by our seismographs. The line at the State Capital is unfortunately busy. Busy all the time!"

"I can call the Governor at home," Miss Pickerell said quickly. "I know his number by heart."

She ran into the room before Captain Crabapple could stop her. She paused only an instant to notice the dust on the large television/telephone console that stood in the middle of the floor.

"If you will connect me," she said to Captain Crabapple, telling him the number. "I will be able to . . ."

A face appeared on the screen before she could even finish her sentence. It was the Governor's wife, wearing a rose-colored housecoat and pink curlers in her hair.

"The Governor is resting," she said, in answer to Miss Pickerell's request to speak to him. "He's had a very hard day. The earthquake you know, Miss Pickerell."

"Yes? Yes?" Miss Pickerell prompted. "What about the earthquake?"

"I hear the people are returning to their homes in Cross Finger County," the Governor's wife went on. "And in Heatherbarrow City, the shaking has subsided. But the Governor says he never saw anything like it. He says he will never forget it, Miss Pickerell. As long as he lives, he . . ."

"What about Square Toe County?" Miss Pickerell cut in, holding her breath and trying to put out of her own mind the memories of terrified children trying to save their animals, of people running on ground that wasn't there, of

. . . "What about the place where the fault is?"

"The place where the fault is," the Governor's wife repeated. "Now let me think. I believe the Governor did say something about a decrease of tremors in the fault area. That's a good sign, isn't it, Miss Pickerell?"

Miss Pickerell did not answer. She was holding on to the sides of the console to steady herself. She began to laugh and then to cry, choking bursts of laughter all mixed up with terrible sobs. And she just couldn't stop.

13

AROUND THE TABLE WITH CAPTAIN CRABAPPLE

Miss Pickerell refused to believe that she had been hysterical even after Captain Crabapple had put his arms around her and assured her that the good news was all true.

"The seismographs in the blue room showed that the tremors were subsiding after you turned the dial," he explained. "I wanted to tell that to Mr. Read, but I never got the chance."

He gently settled her back on the couch between Dr. Donner and Dr. Blitzenkrieg. Dr. Donner, on her left, began feeling her pulse immediately. Dr. Blitzenkrieg, leaning over from the right, passed the back of his hand lightly over her forehead to check on her temperature. And Professor Tuttle directed Er-

nestine to bring some very hot tea with lemon.

"I am not an invalid," Miss Pickerell protested weakly, while she squirmed to free herself from the assistance of Dr. Donner and Dr. Blitzenkrieg.

"You have had a shock," Dr. Donner said soothingly. "Both the temperature and the pulse rate usually change in cases of severe shock."

"It was no shock to learn that a major earthquake had been avoided in Square Toe County," Miss Pickerell corrected him. "It was a relief."

"Well," Dr. Blitzenkrieg amended, "let us say a series of shocks."

"Miss Pickerell can survive any number of shocks," Professor Tuttle said, patting the hand which Dr. Donner had finally released. "She is the most courageous woman I have ever known."

Miss Pickerell leaned a little farther back on the couch and rested her head more comfortably against a pillow. She paid no attention to Mr. Reuben Read, who was rolling in a tea table, or to Ernestine, who was placing a tea pot, a sugar bowl, and a saucer with lemon slices in it at one end of the table and large brown mugs with spoons in them at the other end. And she made no move when Dr. Donner filled up her mug and put the sugar bowl and the lemon slices next to it.

"I have an idea, Miss Pickerell," Captain Crabapple commented from behind his desk, "that my wife's peppermint meringue pie may be a big help. We can all have some with our tea."

Miss Pickerell adored peppermint. Her mouth watered when she even thought about it. And from the way her stomach felt, she knew it was long past her supper time.

"Did you say *peppermint* meringue, Captain?" she asked.

"Yes," he replied, leaning down to take a cardboard box out of the bottom desk drawer. "That is exactly what I said."

Miss Pickerell refused to drink the tea. But she couldn't resist trying a bite of the pie. It was almost as good as Mr. Rugby's eclipse specials.

"I wish I had the recipe," she murmured, as she took a second bite.

"I can give you that," Captain Crabapple offered immediately. "You mix the sugar, flour, salt, and one-quarter cup of water in a saucepan until it's all smooth. Then you beat the egg yolks together with more water, add to the saucepan, and gradually bring the mixture to a boil, stirring until . . ."

"Are you sure it wasn't you who baked this pie?" Miss Pickerell asked.

"I only helped," the captain laughed. "I often do that. My wife has so much to do for the baby, you see."

"Quite right," Miss Pickerell said approvingly. She decided that she liked this nervous young captain very much. She thought that he would probably outgrow his squint as he got older and became more secure.

She brushed some crumbs off her lap and started to stand up.

"Well, thank you very much, Captain Crabapple," she said. "I would appreciate it if you wrote the full recipe down for me, with the parts about the peppermint underlined, and sent it to me. Now I must go back to Mr. Kettelson and my cat and my cow."

"Oh, no!" Captain Crabapple replied, squinting again. "You can't do that, Miss Pickerell!"

"And why can't I, Captain?" Miss Pickerell wanted to know.

Captain Crabapple hesitated.

"Because," he said finally, "I have to make a report about this, about all that has happened today. And I thought if we sat here and . . ."

"You mean a conference!" Miss Pickerell interrupted sharply. "I can't stand conferences, Captain. Nobody listens to anybody else. And everybody has something to say even if somebody else has just said the same thing."

"But Miss Pickerell," the captain said, looking a little baffled, "you will be doing most of the talking. Mr. Read here will take it down on the tape recorder and . . . and that's all."

Miss Pickerell gave Professor Tuttle a hard stare.

"I told you," she reminded him, "that it would come to this, that they would take down what I said on their tape recorder."

"This is different," Professor Tuttle replied. "This is only to help Captain Crabapple."

Miss Pickerell sat back to give the matter some thoughtful consideration.

"I would very much like to help Captain Crabapple," she said. "But I have to see Nancy Agatha and Pumpkins."

"I can have them brought down here," Mr. Reuben Read offered eagerly.

Miss Pickerell thought about this, too.

"No," she said, "Pumpkins gets upset in new surroundings. And Nancy Agatha needs to be milked . . ."

Captain Crabapple lifted his walkie-talkie instantly.

"Someone to milk Miss Pickerell's cow," he ordered. "Outside, near the gate. And some refreshments for her cat and her friend."

He glanced at Mr. Reuben Read, who immediately placed a tape recorder on the low table in front of the couch. Mr. Read also offered to bring in a display screen and a camera. Captain Crabapple decided against both of them.

"Now, Miss Pickerell," he said, "please tell us in your own words exactly what happened. Start at the very beginning."

Miss Pickerell sat up straight and pushed her glasses a little more firmly back on her nose.

"It began, I think," she said, "at the bowling alley."

Dr. Donner, Dr. Blitzenkrieg, Mr. Read, and Ernestine, who had returned to pick up the empty tea cups, all stared. Professor Tuttle winked and called out, "Atta girl, Miss Pickerell."

"The bowling alley?" Captain Crabapple repeated, looking somewhat dazed.

"Yes," Miss Pickerell insisted. "That's where I was bowling for the Bowling for Beauty, Now and Forever Company. But it was really for the . . ."

"I . . . I imagine we can skip all that," Captain Crabapple said, scowling at Professor Tuttle, who was giving Miss Pickerell another encouraging wink. "When . . . when . . . or, rather what made you decide to make this trip, to travel here to Winterwood Forest?"

Miss Pickerell's answer came energetically and instantly. She was glad finally to have the opportunity to speak her mind.

"They did," she said, jutting her chin out first to the right and then to the left to indicate Dr. Donner and Dr. Blitzenkrieg. "They may well be, as Professor Humwhistel told me, very learned gentlemen. And privately, I think they are also kind and most understanding. But I certainly do not believe that they had the right to disappear and . . ."

"Disappear?" Captain Crabapple spluttered.

Miss Pickerell ignored the interruption.

"To disappear and then not to answer Professor Humwhistel's letters," she continued. "They *should* have answered them. Even a picture postcard would have helped."

"We have no picture postcards here," Professor Tuttle said, grinning.

Miss Pickerell paid no attention. She was busy taking the paper napkin out of her knitting bag.

"I followed the dots that Professor Humwhistel and my middle nephew, Euphus, made on this map to get here," she went on. "Professor

Humwhistel made circles and then dots to show me how to get to Winterwood Forest. And then Euphus made dots to show me where the cave was. Of course, everybody knows that deep digging should be done far away from houses and people."

"Of course," Dr. Blitzenkrieg echoed.

"Except maybe the electric company that keeps digging up the streets in Square Toe City," Miss Pickerell added.

"But . . . ," Captain Crabapple began.

"I forgot to mention," Miss Pickerell interrupted, "that Professor Humwhistel knew approximately where Dr. Donner and Dr. Blitzenkrieg were going and Euphus was able to figure out the rest. He knew where the cave was in Winterwood Forest."

"I see . . . ," Captain Crabapple said, sighing.

"My middle nephew is very smart for his age, Captain," Miss Pickerell said.

"I understand," Captain Crabapple replied quickly. "But tell me, Miss Pickerell, what did you know that made you turn that dial?"

"Miss Pickerell already told us that," Dr. Blitzenkrieg stated.

"It was my theory exactly," Dr. Donner added, sighing. "How many times have I suggested at conferences that it was necessary to reduce the water input in a fault area to avoid the possibility of bringing on a major earthquake from the pressure of too much water."

"I *had* to turn that dial down," Miss Pickerell said. "I used the crochet hook from the skirt I'm making for my oldest niece, Rosemary."

She took the crochet hook out of her knitting bag and held it up for Captain Crabapple to see.

"Shall I photograph the crochet hook, Captain?" Mr. Reuben Read asked. "You may want it for your files."

"No . . . No, I don't believe that will be necessary," the captain said slowly.

He looked thoughtfully at Miss Pickerell.

"You remind me of my wife," he said. "She figures things out in her own way and usually comes up with fairly simple solutions to some very complicated problems. And when she believes that something is right, she doesn't hesitate to try it. Miss Pickerell, you have done us all a very great service."

"I should say she has, Captain," a voice boomed out from the corridor. "Miss Pickerell, I have just spoken to Nancy Agatha and to

Pumpkins and to Mr. Kettelson, of course. They are fine, absolutely fine. And . . ."

Miss Pickerell stood up as the Governor entered the room. She stared at his shiny top hat, at his neatly pressed double-breasted suit, at the tan spats carefully buttoned over his shoes, and at the lemon-colored gloves he carried in his right hand.

"Why, Governor," she exclaimed, "I thought you were home in bed. Resting!"

"Temporarily," the Governor replied. "Temporarily, only! You never said, Miss Pickerell, where you were when you called my home. But Euphus knew. He helped me track you down. As soon as I heard the news I came immediately by helicopter to applaud your very remarkable, your absolutely extraordinary heroism."

Miss Pickerell wanted to tell him that he had gotten it all wrong. She wasn't heroic at all. She had shivered almost all the way down that awful elevator. She didn't think there was anything remarkable either about turning a small dial with a heavy #11 crochet hook. But she didn't want to hurt his feelings. And the Governor was still talking.

"I also want to tell you," he was saying

proudly, "that Miss Mina Minor and Mr. Alfonse Quest are now ready to present you on a television talk show. What do you think of that, Miss Pickerell? If we leave at once, you can appear on tonight's program."

Miss Pickerell shuddered and looked around her helplessly. Ernestine and Mr. Reuben Read were applauding. Dr. Donner, Dr. Blitzenkrieg, and Professor Tuttle were smiling cheerfully. It was Captain Crabapple who understood.

"That is out of the question, Governor," he said firmly. "Miss Pickerell must remain here.

She needs to rest, to rest here very quietly for a good long time."

"Near my cat and my cow, if possible, Captain," Miss Pickerell replied gratefully. "They always calm my nerves."

"Mr. Read," the captain called out. "Please put a beach chair outside. On the hilltop. With the animals."

He turned back to Miss Pickerell.

"The view from there," he said, "is magnificent at sunset. Absolutely magnificent!"

Miss Pickerell looked at him sharply. She couldn't say for certain, but she was almost positive that he was winking at her. It was an even friendlier wink than those Professor Tuttle had been giving her around the conference table.

14

A BEAUTIFUL DREAM

Miss Pickerell breathed a long sigh of contentment as she stretched out on the chair with
Pumpkins on her lap and Nancy Agatha beside
her. She would have felt even happier if Mr.
Kettelson had not insisted upon remaining with
her. He sat on a tree stump and began to
complain almost immediately.

"It was terrible, simply terrible, waiting for
you, Miss Pickerell," he said. "The minutes were
like hours."

"They often seemed that way to me, too,"
Miss Pickerell replied, shivering slightly.

"I don't suppose you want to talk about what
happened," Mr. Kettelson remarked, looking at

her hopefully. "Of course, I saw the Governor arrive and . . ."

Miss Pickerell shook her head.

"Nobody ever tells me anything," Mr. Kettelson murmured. "Not even Mr. Rugby, who says that, next to you, I am his best friend. He doesn't even let me know how much he pays for his restaurant supplies. Personally, I believe he is losing money on his half-moon splits. That's a new dish he's added to his menu."

Miss Pickerell nodded absently and gazed out at the sunset. It was indeed, as Captain Crabapple had said, magnificent. The sun, perfectly round and enormous, hung like a ball of fire in the sky. It lit up the mountains and the valleys between the mountains and the tops of the trees everywhere.

"I love sunsets," she exclaimed. "Especially in the summertime, when the days are so much longer. I believe, though, that this particular kind of sunset is usually a forecast of hot weather. It will probably be more uncomfortable tomorrow than it was today."

"Uncomfortable!" Mr. Kettelson burst out. "I can easily say, Miss Pickerell, that today was the most uncomfortable day of my life. You've no idea what fears I had about you when you were gone so long. The first thing I thought of was that you were kidnapped. And I was wondering where we would get the cash for the ransom."

Miss Pickerell did not bother to answer. She was thinking that the leaves in the tree tops would be turning to scarlet and gold in another few weeks. In a month or two, they would be falling down. It would be leaf-raking time on Square Toe Farm. She remembered that her seven nieces and nephews had come to help her with the raking of the leaves last year. It was a windy day and Dwight had worn a navy-blue beret and had tied a striped woolen scarf around his neck. Most of the time, he had stood leaning against the garden gate while he gave instructions to his sisters and brothers. He made sure that they used the wire rakes to pick up every leaf. Euphus and Rosemary had the extra job of transferring the pile of leaves from the wheelbarrow into giant burlap sacks.

It felt good to think about her seven nieces and nephews and to know that she would see them again soon. She turned over in her mind the idea of inviting them to the farm for a week. It would be a nice change for them, just before they had to go back to school. A few days would probably be better, though. With all the noise they made, a few days would undoubtedly be as much as she could stand.

Mr. Kettelson was still talking.

"And then, Miss Pickerell," he was saying, his voice a dull drone in her ears, "I wondered who should be the one to go and pay the ransom. I thought maybe Dr. Haggerty. Being a veterinarian, he could take some big dogs along and . . ."

Miss Pickerell smiled. She adored Dr. Haggerty. So did Pumpkins and Nancy Agatha. But Pumpkins hated getting his anti-pneumonitis shots. And he always seemed to know when she was getting ready to take him to Dr. Haggerty's office. On those days, he climbed up on a shelf where she could not possibly reach him, even with her kitchen stepladder. And he came down promptly at one o'clock when Dr. Haggerty's office hours were over.

"Animals can be very clever," Miss Pickerell said proudly.

"Yes," Mr. Kettelson replied, going on with his own line of thought. "I believe my idea of taking the dogs along to the ransom spot was a good one. I . . ."

He stopped to listen to the whirring of a

helicopter. "The Governor must be leaving," he commented.

Miss Pickerell did not care. Pumpkins's even purring was putting her to sleep. She half closed her eyes.

"I mustn't really fall asleep," she warned herself. "I want to start for home before the sunset is gone. And I won't drive back the same way. I can go through Meadowville and Molesbury."

She remembered how pretty those towns were, with their neat little houses and tidy lawns and low, whitewashed picket fences and gates. She thought about Rosemary, who said she liked paint better than whitewash. She was planning to put a new coat of paint on Miss Pickerell's garden gate. She was going to make the pickets brown and the two posts on each side a bright red.

Mr. Kettelson's voice at the side of the beach chair was rising.

"It was maddening, I tell you," he said. "Waiting that way was absolutely maddening."

Miss Pickerell fidgeted and looked up politely.

"I'm sure it must have been, Mr. Kettelson," she agreed.

She moved a little to settle her back more comfortably and half closed her eyes again. She let her thoughts drift drowsily to Euphus. What a bright boy he was! He knew almost as much about earthquakes as Professor Humwhistel. In a few years, he would probably know just as much. Mr. Rugby said he was the smartest boy in the state. Mr. Esticott, the baggage master, didn't quite agree. He said his oldest grandson in Plentibush City was a better speller than Euphus. Miss Pickerell was not at all sure that this was true.

Pumpkins's purring was growing louder. Miss Pickerell thought that at any moment she might start purring with him. She felt so calm and relaxed and so very sleepy. She had to fight to keep her eyes even half open.

"I'll just close them for five minutes," she told herself. "Five minutes only . . ."

She began to dream almost immediately. She dreamed about Euphus and Rosemary and Dwight and all her other nieces and nephews and about their father, who was her brother, and about their mother, who was always smiling, and about Professor Humwhistel, who was her very good friend, and about Dr. Haggerty, who was the man she loved most in all the

world. She just wished that her seven nieces and nephews wouldn't all talk at once and that they didn't all sound like Mr. Kettelson. She shook her head in protest and opened her eyes. Only Mr. Kettelson was sitting beside her. He was *really* the only one who had been talking.

"You've been sleeping, Miss Pickerell," he

said. "I was trying to tell you that if you wanted
to start for home, we . . ."

"I was dreaming," Miss Pickerell told him, as
she gently placed Pumpkins next to the cow and
stood up. "It was a beautiful dream."

She looked out again over the trees and the
mountains. The sun was slowly disappearing

behind the horizon. But its light still shone on Mr. Kettelson and on the cow and on Pumpkins, who was now industriously washing one of Nancy Agatha's ears, and on the ground beneath her own two feet. How comfortably solid that ground felt now! How wonderful she felt to be standing so safely on it!

"Yes, it was a beautiful dream," she said thoughtfully. "But I'll tell you something, Mr. Kettelson. Being awake is even better."

ABOUT THE AUTHORS

ELLEN MACGREGOR created the character of Miss Pickerell in the early 1950's. With a little help from Miss MacGregor, Lavinia Pickerell had four remarkable adventures. Then, in 1954, Ellen MacGregor died. And it was not until 1964, after a long, long search, that Miss P. finally found Dora Pantell.

DORA PANTELL was for many years an assistant director for the New York City Board of Education where she supervised programs in reading and in English as a second language. She has taught adults and children of all ages for the Board of Education, has prepared curriculum materials for teachers and students, and has appeared on weekly television programs which she wrote and produced. She has also written radio documentaries, materials on illiteracy for the federal government's antipoverty program, films, magazine stories, and books. Her most recent book is *If Not Now, When: The Many Meanings of Black Power* (Delacorte Press). Ms. Pantell shares her Manhattan apartment with her three cats, Haiku, Figaro, and Eliza Doolittle.

ABOUT THE ARTIST

CHARLES GEER has been illustrating for as long as he can remember and has more books to his credit than he can count. He and his wife, Mary, their four grown children, and one cat live in the woods near Flemington, New Jersey, in a log cabin Charles built himself. When he is not bent over the drawing board or the typewriter—Mr. Geer has written as well as illustrated two middle-group books—he takes long back-pack hikes, camps out in the wilderness, and loves to sail.